GOLD MAN REVIEW

ISSUE
14

Contents

POETRY

NONFICTION

Issue 14 Editor's Letter

We've arrived at Issue 14, a milestone for an annual publication, so I had to do a bit of a deep dive on this special number. I discovered that 14 represents transformation, flexibility, and balance. A "letting go of all things out of alignment" kind of digit. I did a lot of that this year.

The biggest one was I let go of my need to be published, this all-consuming, unrelenting pursuit. I think most writers chase this high. We obsess over it on X (or Twitter if you still call it that) as we scroll through agents' and editors' posts to see who's open to submissions, who's not, and what's the latest trend in publishing. We read countless online articles, take classes, workshops, pay for pitch opportunities, and sit through conferences. We're constantly feeding the machine, fueling it with our hopes and dreams.

This year, I wouldn't say I gave up. That's not the right phrase, but what is more accurate is I stopped letting this idea of getting published control me. My dreams needed some breathing room, so I released my death grip and set myself free.

I started branching out into new territory. I joined a book club for the first time, which is surprising since I've always been an avid reader and figured I would have found my way into one years ago. There have been plenty of writing groups in my rear view, but no book groups. My book club is more social than anything, but it's opened me up to work I'd either never heard about or books I told myself I'd one day read but had too many excuses rolling around. It's been hard justifying extra reading time when I could be writing. With the dreams on pause, time became available. Being part of the group has helped me remember why I started writing all those years ago: I loved stories. Enjoying a book just for the sake of it and not to study craft is something I'm learning to do all over again.

Speaking of craft, because I can't help myself, I signed up for some writing workshops via Zoom, a platform I've been slow to embrace. Since I was trying new things, I let my curiosity guide me. Was it worth it? Would it be helpful? Zoom feels so distant, even though it was the platform that helped keep me sane during COVID when members of my critique group pivoted and kept us connected. Maybe it's because it reminds me so much of that time that I've shrugged it off, but this year, I gave it a go. The workshops ended up becoming something I looked forward to as they came around, and since I'd taken the publication pressure off, I was able to relax and take in a lot of helpful feedback. Still, I'll never stop thinking it's weird to see my face staring back at me.

Since letting go of my need to be published, I received two book offers. When the first one happened, I was at my girls' softball game. I didn't know what to think. I'd written that submission off months ago. All I could do was stare at the email, stunned, as parents cheered for their kids around me. It didn't feel real, not even after I received the contract. Then less than three weeks later, the other came from a different publisher for another book that I submitted six months prior. I don't know if there's a lesson there, but I think there is.

What has been weighing on you this last year? For most of the work in Issue 14, it's a bad relationship, a family member, a friend (both real and imaginary), an injustice, or a memory from the past. Whatever it is that's holding you back, let it go. You might just find it's the best thing you could have ever done.

Sincerely,

Heather Cuthbertson
Editor-in-Chief
Gold Man Review

Gold Man Review Editors
Issue 14

Heather Cuthbertson
Editor-in-Chief

Nicklas Roetto
Project Editor

Eric Halpenny
Editor

Kaitlynn Price
Editor

Ashley Rich
Editor

2024 Gold Man Review Reader
Isabel Strciffer

Grandaddy Dim

zac walsh

I'd been tending day drinks at the Open Frame long enough to have stopped counting time, that much is still for sure, or as sure as it's gonna get. Had stopped counting the years too, but I couldn't quit counting uncountable things, like say the amount of deadly invisible microbes crawling around the carpet fibers on those filthy, ridiculous carpeted walls. Because how do you go about vacuuming up the side of a two-story room? And the amount of sporting poses shown in the carpet on those walls that have nothing to do with bowling, or even pool, for Christ's sake. Carpeted walls at a bowling alley, and almost none of the images having anything to do with the game. The beautiful, nearly nonexistent game.

When I first came in here asking for an application, there was a drawer with a stack of forms out of which the man behind the desk would pick your future. Nowadays, if a young person comes in asking for an application, they are directed to that thing called the internet and the Quicksilver Lanes website. The WWW where they can scroll and click and submit their worth through their telephones. Telephones that seem to do everything except teach basic human manners and common sense. But I remember the day pretty clearly, all those years behind me. Only because of my disappointment when they told me I got the job fixing things behind the pin well. Not because I got the job, but because of my learning about the ironclad name tag policy, which states we all had to wear these same polyester collared bowling shirts with the white sideways pin as a name tag.

Ludo—what kind of a fucking woman chooses that for what the world must call her son?

I worked up the courage to ask her about the name, not long after my first drink, sometime inside of junior high. I saw that her Rossi jug was at a good level, far enough down to be easy minded, but not too far down to be fully gone or completely cruel. When I asked her, it was like the name she gave me had never occurred to the woman before. Like my selfish question had forced her to come up with an answer unfairly on the spot.

"Ludo? Isn't that the slob who wants to steal Popeye's lady? The big fat rapist? Ludo, isn't that right?"

Long and short of it is, that when the then manager of Quicksilver Lanes informed me that all employees had to wear the sideways pin name tag with our real names—"no fucking around"—my stomach got poor and sour like it does after a night of too many Fireball specials. And sure, there was a piece of me that said, "Hell, if this name tag thing really is such a goddamn burden for you then go on and walk out. Be a man. Find something else." But I don't know. You ever get that the feeling like there really isn't anything left out there in the so-called world for you in terms of finding? Ever get that bottom of the gut-feeling like if you can't make this basic shit work then you sure can't make something even farther away and better off happen?

So, I nodded my head to the man, and he typed L-U-D-O into his machine that looked like a disregarded child's toy no one buys at the store, and out squirmed a laminated sticker. My identity, my ticket to earn my living. In the years since, I've won awards for consecutive days without forgetting my name tag, which is why some of my older coworkers call me Ludo Gehrig. Which doesn't make it any better, but also can't make it any worse.

Time lets you see it, that is, if you are forced to be still and bored long enough to listen. It lets you see that all the happening, that is happening around you, is just sort of doing the only happening it can do. This persistent feeling that things should all be different is some kind of slow-play scam put on by no one knows, though everyone loves to try and prove they absolutely do. All of it a put-on game by a made-up man I like to call Grandaddy Dim.

Ever since I was a little boy, even before I found the bottle, it was Grandaddy Dim who tucked me in at night and scared off all my goblins. And it was Grandaddy Dim who pushed and pulled me out of bed each morning, tossing off the boulders no one else could see that had gathered over me while I slept. And while it may be true that I held onto this so-called imaginary friend longer than most kids, true that I kept his continuing existence a secret through at least my high school years, I had cast him aside, or he me, about the time I put the work shirt on for the first time. It was as if, having entered into what I often heard called "the real world," he fled to find a more worthy man to protect from all this obligatory light.

The haggard man came into the bar with ease and dropped a league flyer face down on the counter, as if it wasn't strange for a man to wear a tattered black felt suit and matching vest into a bowling alley bar at 11:30 in the morning. On the previously blank backside was this:

LUDO {Anglo} ⇨ *"war, battle"*
LUDOS {Greek} ⇨ *"playful love"*
LUDUS {Latin} ⇨ *"game"* *

When I looked up to ask the all-too familiar man my questions, he was gone, though there seemed to be something like a wake in the air where he once stood, like the kind you see in the ocean during Baywatch rescue scenes. Among all the oddities trapped in this moment was that he, my long-absent imaginary friend, seemed to have aged, as if as my imagination withered with years so did his time-tested appearance. Where he once had thick, blonde-gray shocks of hair, it now fell to his shoulders as pure and thin white, peeling away up his forehead and revealing liver polka dots all along his retreating hairline. His cheeks sagged where there was firm flesh before, and his eyes were less the blue of morning, but more the wolf-ish color of creeping storms. At the bottom of the note, in a hand so small it took a coworker's telephone camera magnifier to read, it said: *The Lydians were the first to make coins as currency. Their originator is called Ludos, a man who said all this is a game board for warlords. Is your mother such a bother after all? Aren't you going to take that call?*

And then, just like no one would've expected, the corded phone in the Open Frame rang and I answered with a loud, growing gong gathering in my ears.

"Open Frame Sports Bar and Grill, this is Ludo. What is this?"

On the other end was a garbled, poorly recorded version of the Popeye the Sailor Man theme song, which I listened to beginning to end several times, each time stoking my paranoia further. All thirty-three seconds of that tormenting tune, anxiously looking for a clue to a problem or crime I was horribly unaware of.

I asked a regular to watch things for me while I had a smoke and rushed out the back exit that looks out onto Highway 93 going east.

Just as I was finally able to light my cigarette with my fumbly hands, I heard screeching and looked up to see, as the first drag of relief entered my throat, an 18-wheeler colliding with a Brinks truck, causing both to hit the center divider and topple, unleashing hundreds of cans of condensed spinach and pounds of gold bricks into the lives of dozens of innocent motorists, who were brought to the mouth of calamity with no warning sign whatsoever. Like looking out onto a sea of pulverized frogs liquified by frozen sticks of polished butter. It was as if my untimely craving to smoke, caused by the hexed note and the all-too timely phone call, had started a bad-tempered domino game on the highway. One started without good human reason, just like a battle, just like a war, just like Grandaddy Dim had always tried to teach me regarding the shitways of the human universe. But now that I was ready to listen, I felt my ears tremble at the high-pitched fear screaming out of those giant rows of melting tires, out of those torn-through cans, out of all the human mouths inside those piled-up cars I could not actually hear, see, or begin to understand.

We live in a garbage can, we live in a garbage can, we live in a garbage can ran in an involuntary loop over and over again in my head. As I walked back in to settle down behind the bar until it was replaced by *so keep good behavior cuz that's your one life saver, so keep good behavior cuz there is no savior, so keep good behavior and wrist clap a razor.* Now there was no voice of Popeye in the sounds careening through my head. Only him, old man Dim. A voice I had not heard since before the morning shakes began to take hold, since the arrogant afternoon slugs at the bar turned to shameful pulls in the kitchen area at work.

As a grade school pariah, I'd spend most of my free time bummed and moneyless at the arcade in the mall, and it was Dim who gave me the lowdown on how to score quarters using only a pocketknife, how to get at the metal fuel I needed to experience what I heard others refer to as "fun." *Use your innocence. Use your scamp. It's not long until it'll be worthless.* It was always that sorta song and dance with Dim, and as I got older it only got shittier, more impossible to ignore. And if you've ever struggled with ignoring something you might understand just fine without me telling you, that there comes a point, call it a nexus or an intercept or really, call it anything you like, when you have no energy left to ignore. All that effort you spent on years of strife with a verifiably unreal foe becomes—like I'm saying in an instant—complete acceptance, like allowing a warm blanket to be draped over your shivering body, only it's over your body and everything else.

My dad showed the most interest, meaning horror, in Dim, especially once I broke down and let dad in on some of what my personal psychic demon was picking up and throwing down to my dad's strange pubescent son. *The gaps and holes, connect them with my strings and only mine, for your father's line is far too frayed.* It was over a game of 9-ball in our basement that I told my dad about what I was hearing with the ears inside my head and seeing with the eyes inside my mind, at which time my father scolded me, "dumbshit," that the head and the mind were two words for the "same fucking thing." And though I knew he was more wrong about this than any other thing I'd heard him say, I focused instead on getting the 2-ball to barely lick off the lower right of the 7, sending it softly falling into the corner pocket like a cried-out baby falling to sleep. *When you finally do wake up from all of this, imagine the relief when your nightmare of wonder is through.*

So it was when the strange day of the smashed spinach and brutal gold came snail-trailing to a close, when day came undone and instead became the night before my 20th anniversary of working at Quiksilver Lanes, my 18th being the conscientious keeper of the Open Frame, I decided to triple-check all the double doors were locked, and tills were safely stored before I set myself up a game of solo 9-ball. Maybe this was in honor of my old man. The bastard did his best. Or maybe in honor of my supposed hopes and dreams or whatnot of nine years ago, or eighteen years ago, or likely just because it was one fuck of a day and pool was always good at getting me to focus on what was directly in front of me, what some like to call "the next right move." And that is undoubtedly exactly what I did. I checked the front doors three times and marked each on my personal ledger, which I keep in my back pocket, one mark for each check of each door. I did the same for the back and side doors. Four sets of doors, twelve total marks. Ideal.

I placed the wooden diamond down, its surface smooth as my face the day I was hired. With the 1 in my left hand, I spun it clockwise with my right until it lost all momentum. I took note of where the "1" on the ball finished as opposed to where it began. Not exactly where it belonged, I spun again, and I continued at this until the outcome of its spin pleased me, or at least this ravenous part of me that nothing seemed to feed since I first awoke from an alcoholic blackout, some morning in a time before any of my friends were yet growing mysterious hairs or had started to talk all cracked up.

Once the ball felt properly prepared, like the host in the hands of a holy and hungry wild man, I lodged it in its lead position five inches in front of the 9. The other balls I allowed to trickle around the 9 and the 1 in whatever order the cosmos deemed fit, like ancient giants, neanderthals and us. Using three fingers and the thumb of each hand, I assured that the balls were firmly snug together, now united in this way for the last time in their existence, pressed up tight against one another like you see molecules doing in high school chemistry textbook cartoons. I carefully lifted the once-organic border entrapping the balls, spun it backward towards my heart, and hung it like a traitor on the ring beneath my groin.

Choosing the cue which felt heaviest tonight, I chalked the tip precisely, not using the drilling motion of a rube, but the scuffing, scraping action of a man who loves the game so much, hears its music so clearly, that he never hums it out. As I lined up my break, letting the perfectly unbalanced weight of the shaft do all the labor, lolling back and forth atop my thumb as if the two together could demand their place in any fine orchestra, I heard his throat clear itself. Turning around, he was there, wearing the same outfit as earlier, now with one of those stock "HELLO" name tags stuck to his coat.

"Hello," I said. "Just in time, I was about to break. Would you like the honors?"

"No, please, by all means," Dim replied. "I've always hated breaking."

"My favorite part, got lots of practice."

My break was strong, but not infallible. Left an opening for Dim to get in.

"Loose balls lift halls," he said as he watched me play a simple low skid, stopping the cue in its tracks and spinning it around itself as the first ball of the game dropped off the table like the pale-yellow sun dripping into the fuzzy green horizon. "Tighten it up," Dim scolded. "Elbow in."

Never good enough, always something to get down about. Even good shit requiring more good shit to remain good, never balanced, never there, never not shit. These things ran through my mind as my eyes squeezed in on the cream and butterscotch target leaning on the side rail, bumming around, loitering, waiting to be sent to its net, nearby and empty.

"What to do about that pesky 3 hiding behind so much trash?" Dim asked. And he was right. My break had left the 3 with nearly no open spot for contact after the 2 was down, but I did what I could to send the 2 home first, to focus on this shot and this shot alone. To do my best, which it turned out was good enough to sink the 2 with a glancing blow and leave my game hopeless from there on out.

"Left only a miracle," Dim said, no longer to me. "Never learns."

"You know what, that's exactly right, motherfucker," I said to the side of the haze, which made up his head, surprising myself.

"A miracle, like the breathless air between God and Adam's fingers holding time against gravity up on that ceiling all these years. You know that number, Dim, right? The one painted for that other full'a shit grandaddy, the guy with the biggest hat in town, that fuck Sixtus? I know you go that far back, can't sandbag me. Not again. And you ever get to noticing what God is floating inside of, surrounded by all those mean, no-good spirits in his head? Look at it, look close. You can do it, you got that kinda reach. See it, Dim? See it clearly? See it like a mirror fully lit up? It's a brain, Dim. A good-ole fashioned run-of-the-mill chunk'a thinking pink. The jobber you wish so bad you had. I nailed it, didn't I, asshole? That's why creeps like you come creeping around nobody's like me, cuz we got what you can't have. A noggin. A cruel, shitty mind unable to be okay and always in motion, after something, never bored even when it feels like boredom. No spirit creeps like you know real boredom, real desolation—cuz at least with a brain and a body you can hit rock bottom and feel what it is to be alive. And that's why you spend all these tiny bits of timelessness trying to upend simple everyday fucks like me. How pathetic for you, Dim, that I get to die, and you don't."

At my meager outburst he shrank, his shoulders no longer broad as the break end of the table, turning him from some kind of tweaked-out matter to merely shadow.

"You have half of it working, as always. A loud-mouthed incompletion, just like the rest of you naive sacks of skin. And yes, we do have interest in you. Verifiably so. You, the ever-uninformed, likely know nothing of my brothers who make themselves all too known all over this dying globe. Thousands of my kind are reported by blatherers just like you—'at the foot of my bed,' 'my limbs were frozen,' 'there was an immovable weight on my chest.' Thousands of you see and report us, moan out to their loved ones, notify the plastic heads on the local news, cry with their fingers into their devices that we exist, that we are here and that we torment those who sleep as our business. But do any of your so-called leaders listen? Do those you hold dear come to your defense? Does anything ever actually change with your kind?

"Sniveling, worshiping, fucking yourselves to death in any conceivable manner. Changing your things so fast you think it is you who are changing. And here we are, coming to wake you up, to do you this immeasurable service of showing you how asleep you really are, and what do we get for it? Derision and disbelief. And you think it is *I* that haunt and taunt *you*? A whole race of beings with so much to offer the rest of the dimensions, yet all you do is scratch at yourselves, more and more violently you tear at your own lives while calling it fine names. Ambition. Gumption. Grit. The naming race. The counting race. The most foolish of all we've found."

At this he exited the room like steam does from a forgotten pot full of burnt oil, leaving behind an unavoidable odor, something between black toast the way my grandmother liked it and an abandoned port-o-john. It stayed thick in the room while I grabbed my coat and headed for the back exit toward my car and the mayhem stretch of highway I bore witness to earlier this day, a day I was ready to never speak of to anyone, not even to these deaf pages. But when I got in my Tercel and turned her over, the radio which was always tuned to one channel and one channel only—98.5 The Banshee of the Bay—did not turn on. So, I pressed the "on" button and pressed it again. Pressed it a third time really hard and juvenile, like pressure was the problem. No sound came, so I cranked the key back towards me and let the engine sit.

In what could've been a few seconds and could've just as easily been a few minutes or more, a voice began to hum out of my barely attached speakers, which were holding on for dear life to the sideboards near my shins. It was a feminine voice, that much was clear from the initial tenor, and it did not take long until the voice demanded to be known without using any words, demanded to tell me it was my mother, that she was there, residing in the sound all around me. In the waves, in the radiation, in theta and beta and gamma hills and valleys in which she had her being, in these and many other formats without human names. Words never came, not one decipherable syllable. In the unaccounted-for time that I sat in my car under the blinking, failing lights of the lot, she told me tales of civilizations that came long before we, nameless, placeless places where the invisible power of sound lifted massive rocks. Belief and knowledge were one and the same. On and on she did not speak, tongueless, and I listened until the dawn broke and long after that too, sat within her hum until my manager knocked at my window until I was awake and told me I was fifteen minutes late opening the Open Frame.

I got out, gave him a hug better than any I had ever been given in my thirty-nine years, and calmly handed him my name tag. I don't remember what I said, but I know what I wish I'd said.

"Turns out there's no such thing as late, Wilbur. Turns out there's no such thing as anything at all."

First Kiss
katie humphries

It was January 1986, in third-period trigonometry, when the Space Shuttle Challenger exploded over my high school in central Florida. Our class, like all classes, heard the news over the school intercom. Our principal's voice, somber and controlled, announced that an accident had happened at Kennedy Space Center. All students were excused and permitted to go outside to observe. Mrs. Lauber, our stern, beloved teacher, was overcome with emotion which stunned us. We were not accustomed to seeing her feel.

After the announcement, Mrs. Lauber sat at her desk in the back of the room and wept. We looked down at our desks with hot cheeks. After a few seconds, she rose from her chair and walked to the front of the classroom. Normally, Mrs. Lauber moved like a gazelle—sharply and quickly—but on this day, she moved in slow motion. She stood in front of the chalkboard and looked directly at us with steely red eyes. "I was supposed to be up there."

She proceeded to tell us that she had made the semi-final round to be the first teacher in space. Something had knocked her out of the running, and now Christa McAuliffe was there instead. Her voice caught at "McAuliffe." She turned to look out the window at the sunny baseball field where students were already gathering, and said, "Class dismissed."

We fled into the winter sun, leaving books, calculators, and backpacks behind.

Students, staff, and teachers stumbled onto the baseball field, united by electricity and fear. From above, we must have resembled frantic ants, searching for friends, boyfriends, girlfriends. There was hugging, laughing, crying. Eventually people looked up. Tendrils of smoke crisscrossed the blue sky and formed a Y. Index fingers rose, pointing at the haze and specks. A hush fell over us all.

Then and now, I prefer to observe tragedy solo. Other people's nervousness and attempts at soothing draws me away from myself into confusion and despair. So, on that day I avoided my friends and leaned against the chain link fence surrounding the baseball field to study the sky. We wouldn't learn until days later that it indeed had been an explosion, and all the astronauts had perished. I didn't know what I was looking at, but it didn't look good. The spaceship and its inhabitants were breaking up and falling to earth—silver smoke and debris dotting the sky—but certainly that was not the truth. Certainly, we weren't witnessing that.

I placed my hands atop the fence, the metal warm and sharp against my palms. I heard breathing to my right. Tim Tucker, from Homeroom and Anatomy, was leaning against the fence. We didn't know each other well, but we shared a mild admiration for one another. We didn't have the same friends or go to the same parties (he was a quiet football player; I was a quiet Yearbook staffer), but whenever we made eye contact, something clicked. He was wearing a sleeveless white tee and black shorts. I could smell his sweat.

"Hey Bagby." This was my nickname.

"Hey."

It got very quiet. He seemed nervous, his presence calmed me.

We turned to face each other. "I was at weightlifting when it happened," he said, voice shaky. He nodded towards the black benches in front of the smoking section. "Coach Bradford lets us lift outside on sunny days."

"That's nice."

"Yeah."

I looked down. "Mrs. Lauber cried in class."

"No shit."

"Yea. Freaked us out," I said, looking back up at him.

"I guess she's not an ice princess."

"No."

Tim's eyes were very blue, almost corn blue, and I could not look away.

He stepped closer and put his left arm around my shoulders. We looked up at the sky together.

"Look," he said.

"What are we looking at?"

"I think it exploded."

Silence.

He dropped his arm and turned to me, all intense eyes and black hair. His face was red. Beads of sweat dotted his upper lip. "I saw the thing blow up when I lifted the barbell. I saw the whole thing."

His voice cracked, and I couldn't take it. I stepped closer until I was just inches from his face. I could feel the heat through his shirt. I looked into his gentle eyes, and without thinking, put my arms around his neck. The charm bracelet my mother gave me for my sixteenth birthday jingled.

We did not smile.

I pulled his face to mine, closed my eyes, and kissed him on the lips. Hard and then soft and then open. He tasted like salt and licorice.

Eventually his body relaxed into mine, and we stood kissing against the fence in front of the baseball field for what felt like hours but was probably ten minutes.

The bell rang, calling us back inside. We ignored it. Students passed by and whistled. We ignored them. Tim put his arms around my waist and drew me closer. I put my right foot on top of his left foot. Lunch smells—tater tots—streamed from the windows onto the baseball field.

We were still kissing after everyone had filed inside and it was quiet once again.

Someone walked up behind me and tapped me on my shoulder.

"Ms. Bagby, it's time to come inside." It was the sound of Mrs. Lauber's calm voice.

I ignored it. Tim tried to pull away, but I clutched him closer. The kissing became robotic, but I didn't care.

Mrs. Lauber cleared her throat and tapped once more. Her finger was cool on my back, and firm. "Ms. Bagby, *sweetie*, it's time to come inside now."

I finally let go of Tim, and we stepped back from one another and stared. We wiped our mouths, adjusted our shirts, and smiled. Mrs. Lauber put a steady hand on each of our shoulders, and walking between us, guided us away from the fence towards school. We walked slowly, with purpose, into the building, never once looking up into the cloudless sky.

Kite
Raji Pillai

The old man sits still, his eyes looking at the ceiling, but not really seeing. He's looking at the past, remembering the woman to whom he was married for forty-eight years. Had she lived, they would be married now for almost seventy years. He had loved her quietly. How else could one love such a force of nature? She was vivacious, her laughter bright and sparkling. She was the life of every gathering. She held court.

From where he sits, he can see the southern wall of the dining room. There are two photos on it. One, in color, is a photo of a man and a woman, with several pots of chrysanthemums at their feet. It was taken when he and his wife lived in a different state. He had always loved to garden, and, in that small flat, he could only grow plants in pots. He tended them carefully, and once, when all the chrysanthemums were in full bloom, his wife said let's have a photo taken that shows all this work you've done, and she made a request of their neighbor, an amateur photographer. She wore a cream-colored silk sari with a broad red and gold border. He wore dark gray pants, a white full-sleeved shirt, and Hawaii chappals. His eyes are smiling, and his wife has her characteristic brilliant smile, her teeth sparkling.

Next to the color photo is an older black-and-white portrait in a carved wooden frame. A young man, his hair brushed back with Brylcreem, has a slight smile on his face and in his eyes. Next to him, a beautiful woman with a gold necklace and flowers in her hair, not smiling. A wedding photo.

Now, it is the year 2026, and the old man is ninety-nine years old. He looks at his wedding photo. It was taken on September 12, 1957, when he was thirty years old and his wife twenty-six. He did not know it at the time, but he now knows it was the day of his greatest good fortune.

Thirty years old. The old man's mind follows the number thirty to another young man he knew a long time ago. That is how old the other young man was in 1936, when he was shackled with chains around his legs, outside a house. The house where the old man lived when he was a boy, in a joint family. Today, there is a brick cell not far from where the young man was chained. A dog is kept there during the day and is let out at night. When any visitor enters the premises, the dog barks incessantly with loud, sharp barks, as long as the visitor is visible. If the visitor is invited indoors, the dog stops barking. Still, now and then, he lets out a low growl.

The old man remembers that the young man had beautiful handwriting. He would write on paper that his mother, the boy's aunt, provided—pages and pages and pages. The old man was a boy, only eight years old at the time. The old man does not know what the young man wrote, or if anyone read it. He knows only what the young man wrote on one particular sheet of paper, which the young man gave him when he was a boy.

On the table next to him, on a pile of newspapers, the old man's phone rings. He does not hear it.

The old man's caregiver approaches.

"Saar, phone."

He does not hear Manoj, who comes over and hands him the phone. The old man brings it to his left ear.

"Hello?"

"Saar, wait, let me answer it first."

Manoj takes the phone, swipes to answer, and hands the phone back.

"Hello? Hello? Aanh, Gautam!"

His son has called to ask how he is. "I am okay," he says. "I did four rounds on the landing with my walker. I also did my exercises, and Manoj helped me. Now I am just sitting here. Yes, I'm all right."

The old man does his leg exercises every morning. Three times per leg for each of the eight exercises. Before that, he walks on the landing with his walker. As he walks, he always recites something in his mind. Sometimes, he recites the poems of Changampuzha Krishna Pillai, whose wife was related to him distantly on his mother's side. The poet and his wife had been kind to him when he was a boy. When he was preparing to go to a different part of the country many states away at twenty-six for his first job, the poet's wife gave him two white trousers that had belonged to the poet who had died of tuberculosis by then. He got them altered to his size. The poet's wife also gave him two hundred rupees. He paid it back thirty years later. (She did not accept any interest; he always notes while talking about it.)

The poet's works were widely respected, especially his pastoral elegy *Ramanan*, a poem of loss and longing, about a dear friend of the poet who could not marry the woman he loved, and on the day of the woman's wedding to another man, hanged himself from a tree. He was wearing a jasmine garland around his neck. This is the poem the old man had been reciting. He felt the poem had a cadence that worked with his steps. It helped him keep count. Sometimes, he recites shlokas from the Mahabharata or the Ramayana. At other times, when he is not reciting verses, he counts from one to three hundred. That is usually enough for four rounds. Then he stops and comes back inside.

He likes keeping count. It helps bring order to things. The old man's brain tackles numbers with ease. He remembers the dates of birth of most relatives—the day, month, year, and even the day of the week. He has been known to use a calculator and then perform the calculation "in his head" to verify it. This is the extent of his ease with numbers.

These days, he has trouble remembering certain things. He knows someone visited him yesterday, but he cannot recall who it was. He mentions to his son on the phone that someone visited. He struggles to remember who it was. Manoj reminds him that it was Jayan, one of his nephews.

"Oh, was it? Aanh, aanh, yes, yes, Jayan!"

He has been taking one pill for slightly elevated blood pressure every morning for the past twenty years, and a multivitamin every night. Lately, he has been forgetting to take them. Now, Manoj gives him the pills morning and night. He does not always know what day of the week it is. He rarely goes out. His sense of the world and of time passing is from the daily newspapers, which he reads avidly.

He is aware that he is forgetting things. He remembers what happened with his wife during her last months, and he knows it is not the same thing he is experiencing. She would see things that were not there. Once, not long after they had moved to this flat, she called out to him and said there was a dog in the room. Why was it there? He assured her that there was no dog in the room. The next day and the day after, she would again point to the same spot in the room and say there was a dog there. One day, he had an idea. When she mentioned the dog, he told her he was going to pick it up and take it outside. He made the movements of bending down and scooping up something, and then walked out of the room, carrying the imaginary dog. When he returned to the room in a few minutes, she was calm, satisfied that it was gone. She did not mention the dog again.

The old man looks around him and his eyes focus as he registers all that he sees. He tries to do this every day. He is afraid that he has forgotten much already and wants to exercise his mind. He wants to keep the mists of memory from melting away.

He looks to his right, through the French doors that open onto the south-facing balcony of the living room. From this vantage point on the sixth floor of the building where he resides, he can see the Cochin Shipyard looming on the horizon, rising out of the coast of the Arabian Sea. The giant cranes are a vibrant red, towering over canopies of coconut palms and mango trees.

The horizon offers no rain, only an unsettling heat from the sun blazing in a cloudless sky. There are four pots in the balcony, in which grow hibiscus, *kariveppila*, and *panikoorka*. A fifth pot has a miniature rose plant, brown, dry. The roses used to be a deep red. Somehow, the plant did not survive. He used to do the planting and watering himself, but now he is no longer able. Manoj does it for him.

M.G. Road, just five hundred meters away, is a bustling thoroughfare traversed by buses, cars, scooters, motorcycles, and autorickshaws, flanked by department stores, banks, the stockholding corporation, restaurants, and shops selling clothes, sunglasses, shoes, ice cream. The din of streets has grown louder over the years, but he can only hear certain sounds and those too, more faintly as the years go by.

Inside the flat, several pieces of furniture rest on the tiled floor. He sits on a wood-frame sofa with three seats. It is long enough for him to lie down and stretch out. At the end of the sofa nearer the balcony is a bolster on which he rests his head when he lies down and reads. It raises his head to a thirty-degree angle from his body. He usually places his right leg over his left, crossed at the ankle. Sometimes, he raises his left arm, so it also rests on the bolster. In his right hand, he holds the newspaper or a book or his phone. His lips move as he reads, silently mouthing the words.

On the coffee table are newspapers, a few from that day, and dozens from days past. To the side of the newspapers, a little white binder lies open, with three chrome binder rings sticking out. The rings hold together a stack of plastic sleeves with several small compartments, each containing a coin. They vary in size. Some are barely a quarter centimeter in diameter, mere smudges of copper. Others are larger, made of silver. Some were from the time of the British in India, a few with the name of King Edward VIII and others with the likeness of his successor, King George VI. They were called the Emperors of India, to signify their sovereignty over India during the British Empire. It is a fine collection, assembled with thought and care over decades, the oldest coin over a hundred years old, from the 1920s. The old man can recite the denominations and their worth. One rupee was twelve annas. He has one that is one-fourth of an anna. The Travancore Rupee is worth 7 panam or 28 chakrams, as each panam is 4 chakrams. He enjoys looking at the coins and talking about them. They feed into his aptitude and love for numbers and for history.

The northern wall of the living room has three paintings, each fourteen inches high and six inches wide, within pale bamboo frames. On the left, Ardhanarisvara, half Shiva, half Parvati. Brahma in the middle, golden-complexioned, with three visible heads, the fourth facing backwards. And to the right, Krishna with his flute. The western wall too has gods presiding over the room. On the left, a brass plate with a dancing Shiva. On the right, a dark metal Ganapati in a box frame. In the middle, the showpiece, the Dashaavataram, the ten incarnations of Vishnu, for each time he descended to Earth to restore cosmic order.

The old man's favorite incarnation is Buddha, who is also his favorite religious figure. By the front door is a cabinet for shoes. The top of it is adorned with ten statues of Buddha, the largest about four inches high, the smallest about an inch. Knowing his love for Buddha, friends and family have taken to gifting him statues, images and photos of the Enlightened One. There are some in other parts of the house as well. He enjoys looking at the Buddhas. Except for a few which are in boxes with recognizable markings, he cannot remember now where he got each one or from whom.

The old man wants to lie down in his bed, rest his eyes. He sits up and places his hands on the handle of his walker, which is red with a black seat, black wheels and handles. Pushing down with his hands, he raises his body slowly. Finally, he is standing, leaning forward. He shuffles his feet forward a few inches and straightens. He pushes his walker and goes to his bedroom. Through the east-facing windows, he can see a Brahminy kite soaring outside in wide loops, its white head and reddish-brown wings striking against the clear blue sky.

He reaches his bed and sits down. Pushing the walker out of the way, he lifts his legs and lies down on the bed. He looks up at the ceiling fan, watching it spin. It whirs with a rhythmic *tak-tak-tak*, but he cannot hear it. When he lies down, he tries to remember things from his past in detail.

The old man remembers the house where he was born. A traditional Kerala house with a *poomukham* in the front, an open area covered by the roof and supported by pillars where the breeze could blow freely. Again, the young man drifts into the old man's remembering. For two years, the young man had lived in the *poomukham*, day and night, chained to the trunk of a coconut tree. A hole had been bored through the trunk and a chain run through it. The chain bound his legs. He could move a little, but he could not leave the *poomukham*. The young man's mother would bring him food.

The boy would wonder why the young man was chained. When he asked his mother, she replied that the young man was mad, and he was chained so he would not harm himself or anyone else. The boy did not know then what being mad meant.

Through his now clouded eyes, the old man clearly sees the *mittam*. The jackfruit trees, the mango trees, the banana trees, laden with fruit. He remembers that the young man was quiet, gentle. As a boy, he would stand some distance away from the young man on many days and observe him. The boy would see the young man writing. The young man didn't look up much.

One day, the boy had just returned from school. His mother and aunts were busy in the house. His father and uncles were still away at work. As he stood in the *parambu*, observing the young man writing, the young man suddenly looked up and saw him, a thin boy, wearing frayed shorts, standing among the trees, a short distance away. The young man smiled at the boy, who walked away quickly.

On another day, as the boy was standing at a distance and observing the young man, the young man looked up at him and smiled. This time, the boy sat down on the ground. The young man returned to his writing. After some time, the young man looked up and held up the sheet of paper, beckoning to the boy. The boy stayed seated. Then, after a while, he got up and walked a few steps closer, then stopped. After doing this a few times, the boy was close enough to the young man to see the piece of paper he held. It was a drawing. *"De, idutholu, kutty-kye aane."* It is for you. The young man's voice was soft, his diction clear.

The boy did not go close enough to take the sheet of paper from the young man's hand. The young man placed the sheet of paper on the ground and slid it toward the boy, so he did not have to come closer. The boy picked it up and ran back to his spot under the trees. He looked at the drawing and was filled with wonder. It could have been a photograph. It was a picture of the *mittam* with all the trees, and in the middle, a boy in frayed shorts, standing with an intent gaze. It was him! No one had ever drawn a likeness of him nor taken a photograph.

The boy ran inside and kept the drawing inside a notebook. He kept the drawing for years, and then, somehow, he couldn't find it anymore.

On another day when the boy came back from school, a similar thing happened. The young man slid another piece of paper toward him. This time, it had words, in Malayalam. It looked like a poem. Later, he learned that it was the opening stanza of the celebrated poet Changampuzha's pastoral elegy, *Ramanan*, which was very popular at the time.

മലരണിക്കാടുകൾ തിങ്ങിവിങ്ങി,
മരതകകാന്തിയിൽ മുങ്ങിമുങ്ങി,
കരളും മിഴിയും കവർന്നുമിന്നി
കറയറ്റൊരാലസൽ ഗ്രാമഭംഗി
പുളകംപോൽ കുന്നിൻപുറത്തുവീണ
പുതുമൂടൽമഞ്ഞല പുല്കി നീക്കി,
പുലരൊളി മാമലശ്രേണികൾതൻ-

പുറകിലായ് വന്നുനിന്നെത്തിനോക്കി.
എവിടെത്തിരിഞ്ഞൊന്നു നോക്കിയാലും
അവിടെല്ലാം പൂത്ത മരങ്ങൾമാത്രം;
ഒരു കൊച്ചു കാറ്റെങ്ങാൻ വന്നുപോയാൽ
തുരുതുരെപ്പൂമഴയായി പിന്നെ!

Forests clothed in blossoms,
Their dense profusion
Steeped in emerald beauty:
An unblemished rustic loveliness
That steals the heart and eye.
A thrilling morning light
Peering over mountain ranges,
Caresses the murky mist,
Nudging it gently away.
Wherever you turn to look,
Only trees in bloom;
Should the softest breeze arrive,
Surely it will scatter down
A ceaseless rain of flowers.*

The old man remembers that he had attended the poet's wedding with his parents and grandfather. He remembers the mouth-watering *payasam* at the end of the feast: there were two kinds.

The old man is a little tired from remembering. Lying in his bed, he closes his eyes. Soon he is asleep. His nap is dreamless. After a while, he awakens. He sits up, reaches for his walker. Pushing down on the handles, he raises his body slowly. Then, standing, he straightens his body and makes his way back to the living room. On the way, he sees that Manoj has placed a cup of tea for him on the dining room table. He pulls his chair out, holds it with his left hand, and with his right hand, pushes the walker out of the way. He carefully sits down. Tea in hand, he looks up at his wedding photo.

The following year when he turns 100 years old, it is the only photograph he will take with him. He will leave everything behind, except for his passport and a few essential items—some clothes, his phone, his tablet computer. He will ask that the photo be taken off the wall and placed in his bag. It had hung in every house he had lived in with his wife. This will be the first time he moves to a new residence without her. He will take her along, in their wedding photo. The albums will remain in the bottom shelves of the cabinets. They are too heavy to take along, and there are too many of them.

He will take a few notebooks. Two blank and three filled with his writings. Three pencils, three ballpoint pens, and his favorite Parker pen, which he always used to sign important papers, such as the sale agreement for the last flat in which he had lived with his wife. He will also take a small box which contained his wedding ring—and hers. And a small orange diary which she had kept, her even, round handwriting on some pages, old letters and memorabilia inserted in others. A faded but intact copy of their wedding invitation in one.

After leaving, he will arrive thousands of miles away. The 100-year-old man will sit in his rocking chair, remembering. From where he sits, he will see *Shantha Samudram*, the Pacific Ocean. Except for the few items he has brought, everything else will exist only in his fading mind. He will see red-tailed hawks soaring in the California sky and will remember the Brahminy kite outside his window in Kochi half a world away.

Today, the old man sits with his cup of tea, looking at his wedding photo and remembering his wife, her smile, her laughter. He becomes a little sad. His thoughts drift back to the young man and he lets his mind take him back.

On hearing whom he wanted to marry, the young man's family was shocked. Who has ever heard of such a thing, they asked. They said it was out of question and tried to reason with him. The young man became agitated. It was determined after discussions with family members and close relatives that he must be mad, mad to suggest such a thing, and mad because he became so disturbed, agitated.

The family considered the options: send him to one of the mental hospitals, to Oolampara or Kuthiravattom or Thrissur. But the patients there were severely ill, physically violent, screaming. It was not a fit place for this young man, gentle as he was, agreeable except in this matter. His mother wanted him near her. She could not bear the thought of him being far away, among strangers. Let us keep him here, she said.

"*Thadi-il idu*," they suggested. Shackle him to a plank. This is what they did at the time to mentally ill people to keep them from harming others or themselves. And the young man was chained to the trunk of the felled coconut tree.

The young man would take a piece of broken glass and carve the tree trunk, rendering it smooth. For his daily ablutions, his mother would bring him a pan. His bathing would be with a wet towel, a *thorthu*.

Nine years from now, sitting in his rocking chair facing the Pacific Ocean, the old man notes that he is 108. That is twice 54. When he was 54, he retired from his last full-time job. The numbers start dancing in his mind. 108 equals 54×2 = 27×2×2 = 3 cubed times 2 squared. It is a special number, 108. The Gayatri mantra is recited 108 times. There are 108 rudraksha seeds in a mala. Rudraksha, the eye of Shiva. There are 108 beads in a Catholic rosary. Yogis practice 108 Surya Namaskaram, sun salutations. Eight years ago, he turned 100. Hundred equals 5 squared times 2 squared if you reduce it to prime numbers. There is order in numbers.

Almost everyone has died. He has lived through a great many deaths over 108 years. He has outlived most people he knew, many of them much younger than him. Before their time, some say. What *would* have been their time, he wondered. What, then, would be *his* time? Again, he remembers the young man who died so young. It is part remembering and part something else. He does not remember the word for it.

The young man's mother took care of him every day, caring for him when he was ill. As time went on, he became quieter, withdrawn. The second year, the monsoons came, and the waters rose. Many in the neighboring village developed cholera. Some died. The young man too fell ill. He suffered for days, his stomach unable to retain its contents. His mother spoon-fed him water with lime juice, some of which trickled down the sides of his mouth. As the days went on, most of it trickled out. His eyes became vacant. Sometimes, he would look at her and say *"Amme."* Then he began looking out toward the road as though seeking someone, something. "Krishnan," he whispered, "is that you? I'm coming."

"*Amme,*" he said. "*Njaan pokatte?*"

May I go?

And she, weeping, held his hand. What had life meted out to her beloved beautiful boy? How did it all come to this?

"*Engotta, monay?*" she asked.

Where are you going?

"*Krishnan-de adutthekye.*"

To Krishnan.

She embraced him, weeping wordlessly. Raising her eyes to the sky, she prayed. *If you must take him from me, give him peace.*

There was a rustle in the *sarpa kaavu* in the distance. The young man turned his head to the sound, then back to the road. "Krishna? Krishna?" The rains had ceased, the air was still. Drops of water clung to the eaves and dropped now and then onto the floor of the *poomukham.*

She wanted to unshackle him. Gently, she put his head on the tree trunk and rose to take the key from inside the house. On returning, she unlocked and removed the chain from his legs.

She gently rubbed his chafed ankles. Her son, who no longer had the strength to rise, to move. She cradled his head and lay down beside him.

"*Amme, Njaan ponu.*"

I'm going.

This time, she knew what he meant.

Holding him close, she felt him draw his last breaths, remembering the baby she had held to her breast, soft, sweet, and gentle. Her firstborn. He was to have lit *her* funeral pyre. But this world did not have a place for him, and here she was, a symbol of the overturning of life's order.

"*Ende kutty,*" she said, "*ende ponnu monay.*"

My child. My beloved son.

Did that really happen? The old man can't be sure. He is suddenly tired. Tired of remembering. Tired of sitting in his rocking chair. The breeze feels a little cold. This is not the warm humid air of the Arabian Sea. It is the cooler wind of the Pacific Ocean. He needs to lie down.

He stands up carefully on the deck, holding his walker. This one is blue, with a black seat, black wheels, and handles. He turns it around slowly and heads inside. He sits down carefully on the bed and pushes the walker a short distance away. He lifts his legs onto the bed and lies down. There is no ceiling fan here. There are vents on the wall from which warm or cool air come out when a dial is turned. He looks at his wedding photo, hanging on the wall opposite his bed, and thinks of his wife. How, after their wedding, they had walked together through the gates toward his house, she for the first time. They walked toward the *poomukham*, where she was welcomed into the family with a *vilakku*, the glow of the wick casting a warm light. She entered the house, stepping in with her right foot. The beginning of their long life together, in many places, many different houses.

Closing his eyes, the old man falls asleep. In his dream, he sees the *poomukham* and the gate. It is dark. Raining. He sees the young man—his cousin—and the young man's mother—his aunt. The young man's mother has unshackled him. The young man slowly rises. He looks at his mother with great love and starts walking. The first few steps are slow, belabored. Then, his steps become steadier, his gait stronger. He gets to the gate, which is now open. Another young man is standing there. The two young men embrace for a long time. They turn and look towards the *poomukham*. The mother is watching, smiling through her tears. The two young men are dressed like newlyweds, with garlands of jasmine around their necks. They smile back at her, look at each other, and hand-in-hand, walk out, close the gate, swing the latch on top to lock it, and disappear from view.

As the old man sleeps, loving hands place a blanket over him.

Translation of Changampuzha's Ramanan *provided by Gita Krishnankutty.*

First Communion

j.a. nicholson

Your mother. The first time she saw me, she was streaming past the back pews towards the exit. Her look entered my eyes and blasted out the tips of my toes. This just after Father Cummins had raised outstretched arms and bid us, "Go in peace."

Saturday evening, Mami had spent an hour crossing out the phone number printed on her glossy white and red cards and writing our current information in by hand. As your mother pocketed one of these, she looked at me again. "Eyes like rays of the sun," she said, and her head shook slowly side-to-side as if this little girl had already done something wrong.

But you were there, clinging to her left leg, silently watching.

Remember?

The first morning on the job, Mami was up with the birds. The mingling of their song and the gentle sounds of her industry penetrated my bedroom walls. As we rolled up the long, winding driveway to your mother's house, near the top of the hill, this little girl asked her Mami, "Is that a mansion?"

But you must remember it, like me, as more of a museum. In one room, statues hacked out of wood that grew in a faraway place stared out in excruciating gazes. From her missionary days. Another room was all sodalite candle holders and exotic gems. Your mother narrated the tour like a docent.

"Don't touch a thing," your mother snapped when she sensed my gaze lingering too long over some display or other, maybe a Japanese *netsuke* or a jewel-encrusted crystal wand. Perhaps the oversized woolen dreamcatcher with feathers. Your mother, she could pull a spirit of menace from thin air, and we were all of us silent as if by a spell.

"Don't touch a thing," Mami repeated in the car while backing out of the long, winding driveway too fast, her eyes bugged wide, crossing herself from forehead to heart and side-to-side. All the way home, Mami choked on the only words she had for the things she had touched with her duster that day or moved so she could pass the vacuum. But the pay was too good, the work too steady.

Do you remember when we were just two little girls, who on paper, never probably should have been friends? The way it should have been: two little girls don't even meet, except the bigger girl will one day want an almond cappuccino with cinnamon and the smaller girl will ask for her phone number, only to credit the rewards points for the purchase.

Instead, up in your room you place in my hands a wooden object about the size of one of Papi's cigar boxes, but without loose hinges that threaten surrender in the indelicate clasp of a child. Your box is smooth, sleek wood. Many pieces fitted together so that the different grains formed elegant geometric and floral patterns. "*Himitsu bako*," your mother called the thing when Mami returned it to her. She hadn't even noticed it was missing.

Remember, up in your room we passed this thing back and forth that had started as a smooth rectangular box? By midway through summer, our small hands had learned these surfaces and contemplated the ordered movements of their pieces. We trained in the subtle applications of pressure that revealed their secrets. Remember tapping the box and listening for clues like old time bank robbers cracking a safe?

Even now, along one wooden edge is a hidden seam where a rectangular sliver slips out of place, no bigger than a little girl's finger. In my hands, the box is evolving into its ultimate form like it did decades ago as two little girls discovered each next move. Thirty-five in all to reveal the lid of a secret chamber. A thirty-sixth to open the final space. We two little girls didn't need to be told what a box like this is for. We had no need for nineteenth century Japan or its samurai with their messages of strategy and strife. We valued only our own secret strife.

Remember how, on mornings when your mother was out of the house, Ruby would pour milk tea for us and lay out a small silver tray of shortbread cookies? Remember how you politely said, "Do have some sugar, dear," when Ruby asked how to prepare my service, and the silence had lingered for a few beats too long? How you would hoist a shortie by one end and then drown it in your porcelain cup? This back when my plans didn't extend beyond preparing for First Communion, but you had already reached the age of reason and received the body of Christ. Remember how you had to stop me from trying to clear the dishes?

Remember you explained your mother believed the whole message of the Bible comes down to a single Greek word the Church correctly translated as "love," though other demonizations translated the word as "charity." Then, in a distant part of the house, Mami flicked on the vacuum cleaner and its high-pitched whistle droned awkwardly in the air between us? My hand went out for the silver tray, and you let your cookie come up for air. The soft mush at the far end tumbled into your gaping mouth. My cookie emerged from below the surface of the warm milk and water but collapsed back into the cup like a stricken tower.

And then you held your hands up with the palms joined in front of you the way Father Cummins did before the First Reading and said, "Let us play!"

You always put yourself in charge of coming up with ideas for games. When you said, "Let's play Daddy Dearest," it meant climbing into the attic and breaking open the dusty boxes where the tape had already started to tear. It meant trying on the scratchy woolen vests inside the boxes and the long cotton pants with gray streaks, like your mother's hair, where dust had gotten into the creases. Remember how we hiked up the waists and folded over the hems and still the pants bunched up over our ankles? Remember how at first, we only put the daddy clothes on over the top of what our mothers had laid out for us that morning?

Even now, many years later, though the precise order of the moves has left my conscious mind, the fingers act on instinct. More pressure in the right places, more pieces slide past each other. Remember how the first time we solved it we couldn't stop giggling? It felt like pulling out roasted brussels sprouts just on the right side of burnt. Then we lie on our backs staring at the ceiling fan until you sat up and went for your sparkly Lisa Frank notebook with a marker stashed inside the spiral. Remember how you wouldn't let me see what you wrote despite all our laughing and cavorting? And then you ripped the page off and buried it away?

"New game," you said, and I will never forget your smile as you handed me the box. "Open this when you get home," you dictated the rules.

Remember?

Even now my fingers tremble with the same anticipation as that first night. After all the lights were out and there were no more sounds from Papi's TV, this little girl slipped out from under the sheet to retrieve the box from its hiding place. Sitting cross-legged on the bed she traced the grains of dark and light wood. You never gave a name for this game of ours, moving the box back and forth between us. Nights when there was a new little note waiting for me in the box hidden in my room were birthdays and Christmas and Easter all rolled into one. In my lap, the box is heavy even though the space inside is tiny and its contents only paper—most of its weight comes from being full of itself.

You must have understood that once Mami found the box accidentally left in my backpack, there were no words to articulate a legitimate reason for my possession. Papi told Mami, "Ask her if she wants to go."

But Mami never did. After dinner, she retrieved an object from the top shelf of the closet in her and Papi's bedroom, something wrapped in delicate paper. Inside was a white baton of wax decorated with a dove set in an almond of gold, facing downward to the base of the candle. A baptismal candle, the wick was already curled and black. Mami confided, "We will light this again soon, for the first time in years." Then she clutched the baton to her breast and gently rocked back and forth longer than usual, her magic a logic of love.

You couldn't have known, but each year we used to take down the photo albums, and this little girl studied all the faces looking for any meaning in the word "familiarity." Mami was looking, too. But we always found the same seas of brown and black irises set in faces more or less the color of burnt sugar. A few pictures had no color at all. Mami would cross herself and kiss the tiny gold icon of the Blessed Virgin hanging around her neck.

The look of your mother, the last time she ever saw me, remember on the steps outside the front door? Even now, the world collapses down to those unforgiving high cheek bones and the unnerving streaks of gray in her otherwise obsidian hair.

Remember the time we were having tea and cookies, how you looked me right in the eyes and said, "Mother is scared of you, but I'm not."

Remember?

Remember two little girls, standing outside the front door of the house. The littler of the two once asked the other, "Is this a mansion?" That inquisitive little girl's hand was still in her Mami's grasp from being dragged up from the car along the stamped concrete walk and the short hill of manicured golf-grass. That little girl's Mami held a rectangular object in her other hand, about the size of one of Papi's cigar boxes.

"*Himitsu bako*," your mother said. But her little girl, the one behind her mother's leg, you wouldn't make eye contact. Or say a thing.

Your mother gave the box a gentle shake but could not possibly have heard the tiny declarations inside. The ones that even now lie on the floor before me, a dream come true. One small, folded sheet with the top edge still frayed from where it had yielded to the coil so long ago, it bears a single sentence in the curlicues of your childhood hand and reads, "The moon and I talk about you." Another says, "Tonight I touched a star and thought of you." Each page evidence of the miraculous.

Out front of the mansion, having surrendered the box, Mami sputtered, "I don't know what got into her head." This little girl tugged on her Mami's hand to gauge how tightly she was still being held. Her words, she tried to use them, and again they utterly failed her.

With a hand on her shoulder your mother let Mami know that there would be other jobs, other friends for her daughter. Sacraments of reconciliation. Your mother, she was finished with looking at me and was already turning back inside. And from her little girl, nothing. Not for some time, though not for as long as it has taken me to reply.

But if you're reading this, your hands at least remember.

Even now, that's all that matters.

Pour Out Like Water

julie johnson

Naomi stops thumb-scrolling Facebook at the photo of an orca plowing through waves with a calf on her nose, sea spray glinting in the July glare. The lede is a heart-blow: *"Initially hopeful upon seeing mother and newborn calf swimming together in Salish Sea waters, researchers now realize the calf died within hours of its birth. Still, its mother refused to abandon her calf, even after the pod moved on."*

Her hand moves reflexively to her belly, cupping a rise barely more than a gas bubble. Eight weeks. Naomi posts a sad face emoji on her friend's shared article and scrolls on.

It's after work and she's sitting on the scrap of cement passing for a balcony in her Ballard apartment building. There's room for a 3-piece IKEA bistro set, two squat terracotta pots with crumbling geraniums and coleus, and Ben's bike, hung by hooks from its front wheel on one narrow wall. Legs stretched across the short, round table, a sweating glass of ice water pressed to her sternum, she bounces a toe against the warm rubber of a tire and wonders vaguely why Ben's bike is here, but not Ben.

Then again, Ben prefers to walk the distance between her place in Ballard and his garage dwelling near Carkeek Park. Cycling demands he pay attention to the world outside his own head. If he doesn't catch low tide at the beach, he trespasses alongside the rail tracks. He tucks in earbuds and turns his back to the oncoming trains, heedless of the danger.

Later that night, Naomi scours the internet for news of the orca—officially known as K23—sucking on saltines until her tongue is burned raw.

"Only 75 Southern resident orcas remain. There hasn't been a successful birth in three years. Although other members of the pod share her burden, the orca mother barely eats or rests. Instead, she glides through the water in the pod's wake with her baby. When it slips off her nose, the mother dives down to retrieve the baby as it sinks, refusing to let the newborn drop beneath the cold, dark surface."

She'd been drinking heavily in the months before she became pregnant. When she couldn't get warm on a late May Sunday, shivering on the sofa, the aroma from the upstairs neighbor's frying bacon drifted down and made her gag, she'd wondered. But she'd been hungover too. She thought to drive the five blocks to Walgreen's for a pregnancy test. It was a terrible thought. One she quelled with a tall glass of icy cold orange juice and vodka.

A week later, she accepted the greasy warm slide in her belly was different than the burning drip in her stomach of hangover acid. First the pregnancy test, then the next day visit to the clinic on Queen Anne. She was six weeks pregnant.

The nurse practitioner at the clinic had tried to sound perfunctory, but she'd glanced up to see Naomi's face, reading correctly that the pregnancy was an unwelcome surprise.

"Do you feel safe at home?" the NP asked. Naomi wondered what systems would be set into motion if she said no. There would be more questions, surely. She'd be given a pamphlet with phone numbers. She would be "referred." What she really wanted was for someone to open a door she hadn't seen. One she could walk through and be someone completely different. Or even just Naomi with no memory of the recent past.

One morning she'd tossed her towel onto the bed after taking a shower. Ben was lying in bed, watching her flip through clothes in her closet. "You have a utilitarian body," he'd said to her.

"Utilitarian?" She'd laughed. She was proud of her body. Years of swimming and yoga had made her strong and tight. She wasn't thin, but her curves were edged in muscle.

"Like a cave woman." He grabbed his weed pipe, a small tin, and lighter from the nightstand. "Functional. Made to bear children and carry heavy loads." He packed the pipe bowl, flicked the lighter, and inhaled.

She stood naked, watching the ritual, too stunned in her shame to respond. This was early on; it may have been the first cruel thing he'd said to her. Not just the dismissive way he spoke about her body, but the bearing children part. She'd already shared with him her infertility sorrows.

"Naomi?" The NP was leaning forward. She had turned her low-wheeled stool away from the computer monitor where she typed notes into an electronic chart and pushed herself toward her.

"I'm fine. Yes. Everything is fine. I live alone," she remembered to add.

Mostly true. Ben is a bassist in an alternative Americana band. He lives in a detached garage of a house not far from Carkeek Park. It's literally a garage, not converted. One of his bandmates' moms owns the house, but with a girlfriend and a sister living with his bandmate, there's not enough room inside. Ben cohabitates with a Mazda in disrepair, sleeping on a cot in the dingy space where black mold eats away at the unfinished drywall and boxes of the bandmate's family's unwanted-but-unable-to-part-with shit.

They'd met in the bougie Fremont grocery store—not Whole Foods but like it—where Seattleites ease their guilt about spending buckets on trendy prepackaged food. Transplanted celebrity Dave Matthews shops there, often with a Buddhist monk in tow. The bald monk, draped in bright robes of saffron and orange that reminds her of Starburst candy, trails behind Dave like an acolyte.

"I heard you can special order monks here," Ben had muttered to her conspiratorially as they stood side-by-side in front of kale and mustard greens, pretending not to watch the musician and the monk. "Biodynamically grown, certified organic. But imported, so…" He made a gesture like scales balancing with his hands while Naomi laughed aloud. They assembled an impromptu picnic and walked along the Burke-Gilman to the Ballard Locks. Then he walked her home.

He's the only guy she's been with since she and Conner split last year. She'd been writing full-time for a few years, found an agent, and published two quiet novels that no one had read when Connor moved back to Central Washington to be with his dad and sent divorce papers via certified mail. She had to find a job with health insurance. Something that paid Seattle's steep rents. She found work as a content and copy editor at the Google office overlooking the Ship Canal. Now she has a 401(k) again, but she's not writing. She's either at work or with Ben.

Ben, who had needed her in a passive, self-contained way that Connor had not. Ben, with his PTSD from his non-combat time in the Army in the early 90s when he'd been stationed in Germany translating Russian intelligence into English. Ben, who hinted that he may have been implanted with a microchip to act outside his will and knowledge, like Jason Bourne.

At work, she sets Google alerts for K23 and Southern Resident Orcas. Outside her window, the air is thick with heat that smells like the bottom of an old barbeque. The normally vivid mountains across the Puget Sound hide behind a curtain of dingy yellow: forest fires have set their blue-green reaches alight. At lunchtime, trapped inside by the chemical taint of burnt air and unable to face the staff lounge, she stays in her cubicle. Eating a container of Icelandic yogurt, she scrolls through the articles her Google alerts have captured.

The entire world is following the whale's mournful progress from the Puget Sound through the Salish Sea. When Naomi learns other orcas from K23's pod have been sighted bringing her salmon to eat, a small cry drops from her mouth. Tears moisten her cheeks, her nose swells, her throat aches. She curls her shoulders and holds her torso, her open palms pressed to her belly.

She read somewhere recently that everyone should have five close friends. A minimum of five. Naomi has Facebook friends from high school in Bakersfield, CA, and graduate school in Ohio. There are a couple of women from work she drinks and goes to clubs with, and some writers she met in workshops at Hugo House that she used to meet up with when she was still writing, humbly admitting she was "forthcoming" and then "published." Before her divorce, there had been the wives of the guys' Connor crewed with on Lake Washington. She lost them in the divorce. And now there is just Ben.

Naomi cannot imagine revealing to any of these women over margaritas at El Camino that she's seeing a man who tells her that he can't stand the way she speaks. That he's broken up with women for that very thing: the pitch and tone of their voice. Also, the way she walks. She turns her toes out, like a dancer. It irritates him. He sounds amazed that he still puts up with her, then hugs her close, kisses the top of her head, tells her it must be love.

She dreads telling Ben she's pregnant. She is beginning to dread Ben.

Naomi swims laps and imagines the orca steering through the cold, salty waters of the Puget Sound, carrying the weight of her dead baby girl for miles. Days on end. After her swim, she's exhausted and can't warm up. She stands under the showerhead at the municipal pool on Queen Anne, unable to leave the hot spray of water. The chills intensify the exquisite tenderness of her nipples. She holds her breasts as she releases them gingerly from her tight suit, one strap at a time—the ache makes her teeth shiver.

The irony of her pregnancy is so perfect, she is tempted to shout out her own headlines on social media. Post one of those sideways selfies on Instagram with her shirt pushed up under her swelling boobs, a hand cupping the tiny round melon of her belly. So, this happened, she'd write. #becarefulwhatyouwishfor

She and Conner had tried for years to get pregnant. The fertility method books, the baffled doctors, the hormones. Until trying was the only reason for sex, and then they'd stopped trying because one more miscarriage was more than she could bear. When Connor told her he didn't want to adopt, wasn't at all certain he wanted a baby in the first place, she began drinking, and then he was gone.

Ben is sitting in that night with a band at The Tractor Tavern. Naomi is exhausted to her core, but she goes anyway. At the set break, she sees him talking with the other band members. She joins him there, punching a straw past the ice in her soda water and lime. Without looking at her or breaking his narrative stride, Ben puts an arm around her waist, draws her in, claiming her. It's the reason she comes to him, willingly, instead of waiting for him to seek her out. Her stomach buzzes in desire and delight at the recognition to the others that she belongs to Ben. Including the gorgeous, petite bongo player with mocha skin and long black hair in wild ringlets who stands alarmingly close to Ben, frequently touching his arm.

His hand brushes over the tiny bulge that puffs at her waist band. His fingers linger, she freezes, he pinches her, leans over and whisper-shouts over the music, "This why you aren't drinking?"

He knows. Somehow, he knows. She imagines she is giving off a scent, something primal that radiates her pregnancy. For a moment, she imagines he will be pleased and proud. They will be a unit, a family, and she will not be alone. But she is afraid to tell him. Knows he will be annoyed.

"I liked your flat belly," he continues. He drops his hand and turns away. Naomi leaves as the band begins their second set. But late that night he comes to her, uses the key she so readily gave to him soon after they began dating, and sucks on her tender nipples until she climaxes in desperate waves. She almost tells him, but he turns his back as soon as he sprays her with semen and is quickly asleep.

She awakens the next morning, a Saturday, to overcast skies. But the clouds are not the billowing dove gray promising rain. They are dull, faintly yellow and within them, the rising sun pulses orange. There is a fine layer of grit on her balcony railings: ash from the forest fires dropped here by clouds that wrap the sky like a shroud, full of sickness. She checks her phone for updates on K23.

"Days after her calf died, the mother still buoys her across her nose in an apparent mourning ritual. Researchers believe this is the third baby she's lost. She has yet to see an offspring survive." Naomi feels hollowed out. Even though a baby fills a physical cavity, nothing rounds out her heart.

They have a weekend trip planned to the coast, a cabin at the ocean. She plans to tell Ben about the pregnancy at some point during the romantic weekend. She pictures clear skies over the water; finally, a chance to breathe clean air. They stop for gas in Port Angeles, Ben driving her car because he doesn't own one, but doesn't like the way she drives. It's not until they stop again in Forks for supplies that Ben realizes he doesn't have his wallet. He'd left it on top of the car while he was pumping gas. She sits helplessly while he tracks down the number and calls the gas station, knowing it had likely flown off on the highway. They are never going to find it.

Ben sits in the driver's seat in the parking lot of a Bank of America branch and slams the flat of his hand into the steering wheel over and over again, the car shifting slightly under the force of his anger. Naomi presses herself against the passenger door, waiting for it to pass. Without a word or a glance, he leaves the car and walks inside the bank. Naomi watches as semis, their flatbeds fully loaded with cut timber, rumble past, shifting the car like the smash of Ben's hand. A couple with surfboards lashed to the roof of their SUV pulls in beside her. The driver, a woman, smiles at her as she opens her door and slips into the small space between their cars. Naomi decides that moment to leave without Ben.

And then remembers Ben has her set of keys.

He walks out of the bank as the woman approaches. He beams a smile and holds the door open for her. The smile is gone by the time he settles back in the car.

"Ben," Naomi says, reaching out to touch the hand that grips the steering wheel.

"Don't you …" His arm flies up and she snatches her hand back. She wonders if his words were meant to be a question or an imperative. She turns her face toward the window and sees the man in the car beside her, staring, his mouth dropped open in shock. He quickly turns away and so does Naomi, her face burning in shame.

They turn around at Forks and return to the hazy, congested heat of the city, the weekend over before it begins.

K23 has let her baby go. Researchers surmise that after nearly two weeks, the baby's carcass has disintegrated to the point that mama can no longer carry it. Naomi disintegrates at the news. Ben had dropped himself off at his garage-dwelling in Carkeek after their aborted trip to the coast, "too upset to be around her right now," as if she were responsible for him leaving his wallet on top of the car. That if only he hadn't been so generous in his offer to pay for gas, none of this would have happened. As Naomi lies in the heat of her bedroom, her shades drawn against the orange stain of sun, she hears his voice saying this, accepts she let him say it without arguing against the absurdity of it, just to get home. Just for the quiet. Here she mourns for K23. Here she lies on her side, bracing her belly against her thighs, craving the release of hot tears.

On Sunday morning, she texts Ben, asks if they can meet at Golden Gardens. She packs a canvas shopping tote with his stuff—the shirts and cargo shorts he'd left, the Cormac McCarthy novel and Richard Siken poetry collection he'd wanted her to read—and straps it to the small cargo rack extending over the rear wheel of Ben's bike.

It's almost noon before he responds that he'll meet her at two. His text is as perfunctory as hers but still she stares at it, wondering as the reply dots pulse if he'll say more. It won't take her long to cycle to Golden Gardens. She checks the tide charts: low tide just before two, she can walk back along the beach.

He's waiting outside the small event pavilion, sitting on a low brick wall, smoking and staring across Shilshole Bay. The mountains are still shrouded, but the cloud layer is blue gray. The sickly yellow tinge has seeped away, the gelatinous sun has vanished. A grove of black locusts, lank and wan from days of roasting in ash, whispers in a current of salty air.

Ben steals her punchline.

"You're pregnant, aren't you?" He chucks the cigarette butt to the side and stands to face her. She hears the tinny screech of a guitar coming from the ear buds that dangle around his neck.

She opens her mouth, then closes it, gripping the handlebars of his bike so tightly her fingers prickle with pins and needles. She watches as the still-burning butt releases a trail of smoke into the fragile air.

"I'm sure your insurance will pay for an abortion."

Naomi slowly pushes his bike forward until the front tire connects with his knees. She gives it one final shove, then releases the bike.

The last thing she sees of Ben: his arms flying out, his legs jumping backwards. The last thing she hears: a simultaneous clatter of metal against cement and a hissing string of curses. But she turns and walks away. The breeze picks up and pulls her to the shoreline.

What Naomi neither sees nor hears in the moment, she chances upon a day later while scrolling through *The Seattle Times* at work.

- K23 was spotted of the coast of Vancouver Island with her podmates on Sunday, leaping from the Salish Sea in pursuit of a school of salmon.
- A low front pushed in off the Pacific, dousing the Olympic Mountains with rain; it is moving steadily northeast, the rain keeping up with the wind, to soothe the scorched Cascades.
- A man, walking a bike across the BNSF tracks, was struck and killed yesterday afternoon by a northbound Sounder commuter. Witnesses say he had his back to the train and ignored the horn and the squealing emergency brakes.
    - ° BNSF reported this as the 12th fatality on its tracks in the state this year.

The Boy Who Fell from the Sky

elizabeth duran

It was a peculiar morning. Though the sky was majestic purple with hues of cyan drenched behind the clouds, it was peculiar to say the least. The sound of the beach was a quiet reminder it existed. As the fastidious morning swept itself into midday, the peekoos pressed themselves into the wind, and dipped their wings in a gentle manner. They glided across the sky, and without warning, dropped straight down with the same graceful force, where they landed with a splat against the cold, hard ground.

Little Tommy, who was seven at the time, curiously walked over, and after a bit of hesitation, scraped one off the ground. He scooped up as much of the bloody goop into his palms and ran to show his mother, who was nowhere in sight. It was just him, a freckled, dark-haired child with cerulean-tinged cheeks. He stared at the dozens of red and black swirled imperfections scattered around him, and he held his posture steady as he moved gracefully around the fallen peekoos.

He was quite stable and mature for a seven-year-old, and so he composed himself and walked to the nearby beach to cleanse his hands. He placed the peekoo in the ocean and tenderly began to rub the rocks, dirt, and blood from its tiny feathers. Its beak was twisted and broken, and he removed it by effortlessly cracking it off the bird's face. He placed the peekoo into a white handkerchief, wrapped it with care, and put it in his pocket. Perhaps, he would show it to his mother when the time was right.

He peered off into the ocean, losing himself to the endless push and pull of the waves. He squinted through one eye at the miraculous glow of the sun and tried to catch it between his fingers. He ran into the ocean until his knees were submerged and trudged about in a playful manner. When he was ready to go home, he felt around the outside of his pocket, until he gently touched the tiny knot and glimmered with a renewed hope.

On his way home, he looked up to spot the peekoos, but none were left. Not one *caw* to guide him home. This made the boy sad, because it was entirely possible that all the peekoos had perished that day.

He returned to find his home empty. The familiar scent of baking bread was missing. The sound of his mother's lovely humming had also been misplaced. The home was just an empty house overlooking the beach below. He observed the way the cliffs hung above the ocean, as if they themselves peered into the great puddle below.

He sat on the floor and placed the small handkerchief under the light shining through the window. He stared at the mangled peekoo and rubbed what was left of its chest. Its neck was broken, and its hocks were stiff and pointy. He went outside and plucked some leaves, branches, fruits, flowers, and anything else he could find. He took a ruby red quizzle and squeezed all the pulp out of it. He soaked the leaves in the juice and dressed the peekoo into a scarf that held its head up. It appeared peaceful-like, as if it were only sleeping. He broke off pieces of the branches and replaced the hocks with useful claws. When he was satisfied with the peekoo's appearance, he made a blanket out of the remaining leaves and tucked it into bed. The boy slept next to the peekoo. He would wake often to check on his friend, and when it was morning, he took it and placed it in his hand and admired its elegance. He cupped the bird in his hands and gracefully fluttered him through the sky the way any peekoo would enjoy.

The boy ran to the highest cliff overlooking the beach. If he could get him high enough, he could send the bird flying one last time. A familiar feeling swept through him, and he looked down at the ocean below as he held the peekoo up to let the bird see things as he did. He held the peekoo up to his ear and listened to what the bird needed from him. The boy nodded and together they fell from the sky and flew. The wind cut through the boy's hair. He laughed as it tickled his body. He held his peekoo in the palms of his hands, and when their bodies approached the bottom, he kissed it, and together they splashed into the great body of water with a squelch that quietly echoed.

The boy wallowed; the peekoo wallowed; the warm, crisp air danced above the pleasant current as it innocently swayed them to land. That is when the boy set his sight on the oddest thing. It was a miniature crab facing the sky. Its legs—desperate for land—had begun to tire from all the strain of trying to get right-side up again. The boy took out his finger and tickled the crab's underbelly gently, but the crab was too exhausted to fight, and instead it let out the most curious sound. A hollow whimper of acceptance.

Unsure of what the sound meant, the boy showed the crab his pee-koo, which was still fashioned with twigs and berries, and he slowly scooped up the crab tenderly into his hands. The boy studied the crab's shell. It was cracked and partly smashed, but the crab was calm and wide-eyed as it balanced himself proudly in the boy's grasp. The boy walked along the beach content with his new helpers, and when the day had outgrown its welcome, and his exhaustion had matured, the boy returned to his empty home once more.

Later, he picked quizzles and laid some out for the crab, but the crab did not eat, instead it stared at the boy in an unusual way. It swayed its head curiously. The boy yawned and fell asleep as he watched the crab stare at him in wonder.

On the third day, the boy awoke to find the crab and the peekoo gone. He searched the entire home and the beach but found neither. For the first time, he felt alone, and the sting of emptiness pressed heavily against his chest. That night, he lumped himself into a ball and slept on the floor in the kitchen unsure of what would happen next.

As he slept, he was awoken by the desperate sound of a mother's plea. He opened his eyes and smiled as his eyes focused on the sight of the peekoo. It was wonderfully perched on top of the crab, and the crab stared at the boy as it continued to make the unusual sound. The boy rubbed his eyes. "Mama?"

The crab began to travel. The boy began to follow. And the three of them made their way towards the sound of his mother's voice.

Clutching My Pearls

r.g. mint

My husband was a great man when we met. He was chivalrous, generous, and loyal beyond any doubt. And it was because of his good nature that I fell in love with him. It was even more so why I agreed to marry him all those years ago. Like other delicate things, our marriage was new and marked by his finest gift to me—a string of exquisite Tahitian pearls, pink as rose milk.

"For you, Diane," he had said that day. And I was his.

The years weathered us, as they do to every marriage, but the pearls always maintained their luster. They even became a pillar of my pride. Friends would remark that if an event were formal enough, they would no doubt see me donning my beloved pearls. I would visit them, alone and unbothered on a black velvet bust, each morning as I dressed. Nothing else could sit next to them for they were the finest trophy and had earned their solitary place in my boudoir. Earring, rings, and necklaces kept company with each other in their jewelry boxes, but the pearls were always on display, symbolizing the contract of love between me and my husband. I loved my husband, and I loved my pearls.

It was on a morning like all the others when I made the discovery. Normally I would wake, prepare breakfast for my husband and our three beautiful boys, and hand my husband his briefcase before kissing him and wishing him well on his day's work. My attention would then shift to my sons, who would wrestle each other to my great chagrin, grab their school bags, and leave precisely thirty minutes after their father to catch the school bus. Then, my day became an opportunity.

Opportunity to phone a friend and gab over coffee and sweets. Opportunity to launder the week's dirty clothes or run to the supermarket and get the fixings for each meal over which my family would dine.

But this morning, something was askew, and I hadn't noticed until I sat alone in my empty house. In the morning's bustle, I had callously forgotten to hand my husband his briefcase. So silly of me.

He always kept it on his side of our closet. I never commented on his slapdash tidying habits, nor would he remark on the pristine order of my finely tuned and cataloged wardrobe. We crossed into each other's territories only when directed. And each morning, he would be a step out of the doorway when he would turn to me in frustration and scream at me for his briefcase, at which point I would retrieve it, wipe away my tears, and kiss him goodbye, his kind smile returning as he walked to his car.

The anxiety pinched me as I wondered what he might do now since I had forgotten his briefcase for the first time. The boys had already left, their minds focused on the homecoming game and applying for scholarships. I dashed into our closet, grappling for his briefcase. The worn thing barely kept itself together at my touch. I would have bought him a new one had he asked. Grabbing it and rushing to the phone, I wavered as the briefcase couldn't maintain its composure and broke open when I set it down.

Inside, the expected ledgers and documents splayed out as disorderly as my husband's side of the closet was arranged. Decidedly out of place, I discovered a dainty rectangular box, a sky-blue eyesore wrapped in felt.

What was the day? Was our anniversary approaching already? Oh, I had surely forgotten. I opened the box to see a small string of pearls, not pink like mine, but a polished ivory color, something neutral. It was a less striking gift than my original pearls but appropriate for casual wear. I had already started matching the new pearls with outfits in my mind when I noticed a little note that had fallen out of the box when I opened it. *For you, Alice*, the note read.

Dropping the box, I lurched toward the telephone, dialing his work.

"Fairview Finances, this is Alice. How may I help you?"

I slammed the phone down on the receiver. Curling up on our cherry wood flooring, tears streamed down my cheeks, and unlike all the other times, they could not be stymied. When my husband screamed in my face for doing something wrong, I would only cry in secret. When I would make a mistake with his meals, and he would call me horrible names, I would at least refrain from crying until after the food had been served. And when our boys were in bed after I fed and bathed them in their early days, he would climb on top of me smelling of his favorite liquor, and I would cry only after he had fallen asleep. But these tears were not like the others.

The thought of what would happen next quickly struck me, my regimented mind's only coping skill when grappling with this betrayal. I could have called the accountant, but he would have confirmed what I already knew—the house, car, and money were all in my husband's name. Nothing was my own. I cried until I was reminded of my only comfort. *My* pearls.

Picking up and tossing the gift for Alice across the room, I collected myself by picking up the briefcase and slamming it against the wall on his side of the closet. He would never notice it was moved at all. Then I clutched my beautiful pink pearls and removed them from their stand. Unlatching the necklace, I draped the string around my neck, fastening the back with a metallic clamp. I looked radiant in my pearls.

The rage flared on my face, reflecting at me in our mirror. A face tired and worn from mothering and wifely duties. Not an ounce of authority, but yes, I had my pearls.

Pearls which I now hated. The pink ran red as blood in my tunnel vision, the shimmer muted. He may leave me the house so I may raise his sons, but what then? They were all three going to graduate within the year and leave us, and the house could become a love nest for him and Alice or whichever woman he desired. They got pearls too, but none of his vitriol. None of the harsh words or guilting glances.

My parents were gone just as his parents were, and my sister still refused to talk to me. Our squabble over our parents' funerals had proven unmendable, and we lived estranged from each other. Perhaps a girlfriend could take me in, but then they'd know the truth. I'd owe them an explanation, and that wouldn't do. And what would I tell the boys? I couldn't bare the truth to them, but I also couldn't stomach what sweet lies their father would pour into their ears about his infidelity. And they idolized their father. They'd believe whatever he told them.

My hands shook as the rage intensified. I loved my husband, and I loved my pearls.

Wearing my favorite treasure, I sat on the closed toilet and continued crying on a seat that should never have been where it was. I had asked the day we moved into our house for the master bathroom to be extended. I explained very pragmatically how the tile floor didn't match the aesthetic of the rest of the room, and the toilet was far too close to the shower and the his-and-her sinks. There had always been too much risk. A splash of water and one of us would fall. But his confidence and authority overruled my concern. And with his brazen acts with Alice, it seemed my voice had only ever been fleeting whispers and nothing more.

I ruminated on how to spite him. He spent years placating me with pearls and jewels, but those were easy for him, as verified with his gift to his receptionist. He had only done such acts to keep me docile and under his thumb. I could burn down the house or drive his car into the lake a mile outside of town. It would be years before they found it.

But no, I hadn't my husband's steely resolve to do anything of the sort. I would sit and remain obedient to him and his whims as he had always wanted me to. I ripped the pearls from my neck. A swift motion exploding into a shower of pink marbles, each bouncing off the out-of-place tiles and scattering across the bathroom.

My pain bent me over the counter top, and spittle dripped from my mouth and nose, mixing with the tears that had already fallen. The watery mess dropped into the sink. Shrunk to the floor, I collected each pearl that had brought me so much pride in my marriage. Each was stowed in an empty drawer, harvested like legumes from the soil. The count was lost to me when the front door opened and closed. I knew the sound well, having heard it every day when my boys tumbled in after football practice, followed by my husband, who arrived at the precise time I placed his steaming dinner on the table.

But the boys had a game today and would be gone all evening. And they knew certain grounding awaited them if I found them skipping school. It was my husband, here for his forgotten briefcase. I endeavored to collect as many pearls off the floor as I could and stash them away before rushing out to the armchair in my bedroom, where I always read my books. Before he entered, I managed to wipe the appearance of distress off my face, but it, of course, lingered under the surface.

"You forgot my briefcase," my husband said, his face awash with enmity.

"Your tie is crooked," I told him to change the subject. "Here, let me fix it for you."

He waved me off before I got to him. "Shouldn't you be with Lisa? I thought she needed help with the fundraiser today." He removed his suit coat and laid it across the bed. He had gone nose blind to it, but the scent of floral perfume wafted from it and nearly made me sneeze. Alice had a dismal taste in perfume, it seemed.

"Oh, yes. I'm…uh, meeting her at the women's shelter. We'll probably go well into the afternoon. I have a casserole in the fridge you can heat up after work. Then you can meet me at the boys' game."

"Won't be there," he said, combing his gelled hair. "Tell them I had to leave for a work thing but that I caught most of it. Those games are always the same. Besides, I'm meeting some work friends at the Sheraton for drinks. I'll eat there."

The hotel bar he frequented after work with his associates. It all became suddenly clear.

"I'll tell them," I said, avoiding his eye line.

"Go, I don't want to hear from Lisa that I was the reason you were late." He stepped into the bathroom to relieve himself, the heavy stream undoubtedly splashing urine and toilet water on the floor that I would inevitably have to clean. I grabbed a wrap from the closet—the chilly nights during a football game would nip at me otherwise—and picked up my purse to take my leave. The women's shelter felt like the ideal option for me regardless of the fundraiser, but I welcomed the distraction, fleeting though it may be.

I tensed at what was to happen next. He would take his briefcase to work, find his surprise for Alice missing, and confront me in a white-hot rage. Maybe he would even open the thing here and whip out of our room in a fury, yelling in my face while I told him how I loved him and forgave him regardless. But I didn't forgive him, and no such acrimony came for me.

I reached for the door, content to get in my car, leave for the fundraiser, and confess to Lisa how my life had changed instantly when the strangest sound rang through the house. A fleshy slap against something hard reverberated from the master bedroom. It sounded as though someone had slammed shut a toilet seat or thrown one of my finest dishes against the wall. The groaning came next, but I stayed where I was, the knob of our front door firmly in my grasp.

The sounds were my husband's voice calling for my help, but the language he used was stunted and guttural like someone had removed his tongue. Concern welled for my husband's safety, but again, my body refused to move. More clamoring echoed, and I waited attentively for what would follow. I imagined my husband, his hair muddied with blood, staggering out with a towel pressed to his head, telling me to call an ambulance through his slurred speech. Or he would sprint out of our room and strangle me where I stood for not warning him about our narrow bathroom more frequently. But I had warned him. So many times.

That morning was so full of mistakes.

It dawned on me that, fearing his unexpected reappearance, I may have forgotten to pick up a pearl or two. It was a tragic error, and I felt sorry for the whole thing.

The noises from the bathroom ceased, and I stood frozen in the silence for quite some time. A dangerous amount of time, one might have said. But Lisa needed me at the fundraiser, and I couldn't forget my boys. It was their championship match, and at least one of us had to be there to support them.

I called for my husband, his name bouncing through every corner of our home. No reply came, so I tried again, and the house remained still and quiet. A curious feeling sparked in me then. I didn't know what it was as I waited there in reticence until it struck me like a blow to the head. It was a feeling I stumbled upon every day when my house was silent, and I was alone. Opportunity.

The entire trajectory of my life pivoted to countless opportunities. When I returned home from the women's shelter and the boys' game, I would find him and, in my horror, call the police, weeping at the bloody scene in my cramped bathroom. His work may have phoned to ask why he never returned, but I had been helping a friend with her fundraiser and went straight to the football game, and it wasn't as if he could have answered.

Next came the stress. The mourning period remained inevitable, with funeral flowers scattered across the living room table and the constant need to sweep up wilted petals. So much planning was involved, but even in my tragedy, opportunities awaited. I could have people over as often as I wanted, and they wouldn't refuse a newly minted widow.

I thought of the tragedy this would bring on my sons but was assured my love alone would be enough for them to endure. It might even be a tragedy that brings us closer together. I had birthed all three on the same day, after all. And they'd soon be off to college to live their own lives, returning to me for holidays with new girlfriends or wives or little children of their own. I needed to be there while they needed me. Then, I would have the house to myself to do what I wished.

The coroner would clean the mess, but it was doubtful the blood hadn't stained the grout, so the tiles would need to be removed. The room would also need to be expanded, and the toilet would need to be moved to avoid any recurrence of sloppy accidents, but without my husband, I would be granted the means to pay for it.

My last minutes in the house were spent contemplating if I should have helped him, or at least attempted to, for what was found of him later that evening was a bloody mess beyond saving. A skull so perfectly cleaved against a toilet that no one would question it as anything other than accidental.

I wiped my face for expected tears, but there were none. Instead, I felt the tightness of a grin, for a final idea occurred to me. Everything was in order, save for a little blue box under my dining room table, launched from my hand in a rage. It needed to be dealt with before my departure. Opening the rectangular box, I coiled my fingers around the new pearls and reminisced on their unintentional gift. Having endured what I had endured, I ripped apart the note to Alice and donned the necklace meant for her.

I loved my husband, and I loved my pearls.

POETRY

Taste of Temptation

maria l. berg

While cutting around the brown, soft spot
in this small, orange pepper,
I realize I'm still angry
at the rotten apple from two nights ago.
Why am I so angry at the apple?
Not the store that sold me rotten fruit.
Not the moldy taste that lingered
which seeped into the white flesh
I thought I could eat, or the fear
of feeling ill after tasting it.
No. Today, as I cut the brown spot out of the pepper,
chopped up the rest, and put it in the skillet,
I was mad at that apple for seducing me,
making me believe it could sate my hunger
with a reward both sweet and crisp,
a treat before falling off to sleep,
but then the bait and switch,
the surprise betrayal,
making me suspicious
of all the apples in the bag.

Bourbon in My Latte

saundri luippold

When there was bourbon in my latte,
And we both wore white and green,
When there was cinnamon in your chai,
And we stepped in sync, serendipity.

The bourbon in my latte dizzied my balance,
scripted daydreams, directed reality.
I can't drink bourbon in my latte,
I'm only 19. I have to drive myself home.
So you suggested we trade drinks,

My stability faltered even more.
The taste of your lips wavering over me,
They taste like Fall, my favorite season,
They taste like freedom, my sweet escape.
Captured on film, the ink fades away.

When there was bourbon in your latte,
You held me up when I was about to fall.
When I drink from your cup,
I become more drunk.

Maybe our shared bourbon distilled our fate.
Maybe the bourbon in my latte opened a forbidden gate.

Advice for Fishing the Coos River

zachary paul

If Dad picks you up at school and says the Suburban died, don't
worry. He will ask Mrs. Button for a jump, she will hop into the air
and they both will laugh. The drive from TNT Market to the boat
ramp is just enough time to pick the first handful of Jujubes from
your teeth. Heading upriver the wind will be cold. There is a warm
spot tucked beneath the steering wheel. When the boat stops, find
the cooler. Under the bottles is a silver can of Diet Pepsi. It still tastes
good. Other boats will pass and camouflaged men will hold up some
fish - cheer as loud as you can. If you have to pee, you can go right
over the side. It's fun. Just tell Dad and everyone will look the other
way. Dad will move away soon, but it's okay, he is just a few towns
over. You can see him every other weekend. The boat will look far
away from the dock, but it really isn't, you can just step right off. It
won't feel like you did much, but on the ride home you will get real
sleepy and nap. You'll wake up twenty years later, see a red handle on
some jumper cables and wonder if Mrs. Button is still alive. People
will occasionally ask about your hobbies and you can say, "I haven't
been in a while, but I love to fish."

One of Everything

kirk glaser

We freeze under fluorescent lights
dangling on silver chains,
rows of tubular suns coldly aligned

over aisles of drugstore goods.
"Can I help you?" a red-shirted girl asks,
silver ball bobbing on pierced tongue.

"We need one of everything." The girl
narrows her eyes. "I'm sorry?" "Not everything,
we have a toothbrush, just everything else."

The fire has glazed our humor like this,
pigment too dark for a high school girl
just saving up for her next tattoo.

Maybe she thinks we are among those
who rise from the river banks
each morning, crazy, lost, or damned

unlucky, wandering in for bandages,
juice, a jug of wine, alcohol wipes
to clean a needle and face another day.

"It's okay, we'll find what we need."
The girl walks away, leaving the question,
what do we need? Two minds pull me.

One set to fill our home again
with the myriad things that anchor a life.
The other on scent of a path burned clean,

tracking Muir through the Sierra range,
a crust of bread in his pocket,
cut fir boughs for a bed.

Or Basho leaning on the staff of an ancient,
leaving his ramshackle hut by the river to gather
emptiness over a thousand leagues.

Three Untitled Haiku

cassady o'reilly-hahn

The angriest vines
        close their fists around boulders
as if to throw them.

In Los Angeles
        the grey hairs of our giants
are made of freeways.

In my father's eyes
        the foot of the crow has perched
in its longest spring.

Walking in the Dark

faith allington

At the highest point in Cook's Cove,
rainwater pools in every crevice and ditch.
Grey clouds break, sunlight pierces like gold
and wind drives us to our knees,
our palms pressed to moss and grit.

Tongues of foam and water glide
across the shore, rocks glinting
in their wake. Two deer slip between
nearby houses like ghosts.

We spend hours gathering and preserving
stories until dusk stains the sky.
Copper-fletched, shadows lengthen
and fall. Suddenly, the whole world tips
into night. As we walk home, I scry
an alchemy of futures under crowding trees.

By darkness, the calling of dogs
turns monstrous. My body ignites
with the fear of what might be following,
the thought that even in a hundred years
our bones will be so small and new
in this ancient landscape.

Dead end

e. peregrine

Farther down this familiar road
than I ought to be, again,
wheatstems and burs cajoling
my calves, a hundred
no trespassing signs of my very own
as if that has stopped me before.

I know not to be here.
I know to pick the debris
out of my socks before I blister,
to name the thoughts as they come
and do away with them, distract
myself until they've gone, outsmart
the hooks and spines
of wayward neurons out walking
where they shouldn't be either.

I have compassion for the burs.
They must go so far or perish
in a mess of wildflowers
everyone loves more.

NONFICTION

The State of Grace
hannah andrews

I discovered my family tree recently. My original one. My long-lost biological one. I began excavation immediately and unearthed roots riddled with shame and secrecy. No surprise, really. My adoptive lineage had its angst and the un-spoken ofs too, but those dissipated with time. Elders often offered full disclosure in their golden years, sometimes with sighs, sometimes with giggles. Just a part of life. I was eager to dive in. I wanted to duct-tape my broken branch right back on, even more so once I heard about Grandma Grace.

In 2019, I discovered Illinois had amended its law regarding adoptee's access to their original birth certificates (OBCs). Initially sealed in supposed perpetuity, a portion of my birth records were now legally available to me. With infant adoptions in Illinois, records are locked away and a new birth certificate is issued with the names of our adoptive parents listed "as if" we'd been born to them. Legally erased and replaced. So sketchy. Still, I sent for mine, then began a fever-pitched search for my biological mother. That search ended a year later with a gut punch of a revelation that she'd died a decade earlier, at age 55.

It also introduced me to my half-brother, her son, a warm and welcoming man 18 years my junior, who lived just twenty minutes away. His was the first face I ever saw my own in, the first blood relative I'd ever met. *But wait,* fate teased like a cheesy game show host, there's more! In the middle of our get-to-know-you lunch, my new kid brother surprised me with a photo of our grandmother and said, clearly and in the present tense:

"I haven't decided whether to tell Grandma about all this."

My heart leapt.

"Our grandmother is still alive?" I began silently plotting. I'd grab his phone, run to the washroom, and dig for her number—likely under G for Grandma. I'd lock myself in a toilet stall and call her. But he skated around my thin ice of a dream, said something about not knowing how she'd react, how she was stubborn. I stopped listening.

"Sure, I understand," I lied.

Maybe it was greedy of me. I'd already had two amazing grand-mothers, the mothers of my loving late adoptive parents. Dad's mom, Nolena, rolled out homemade egg noodles (even though they cost maybe fifty cents at the Piggly Wiggly) until her dying day. She was hardscrabble, but pampering. Ethel, my Mom's mom, refused to let anyone but me read her Guideposts stories aloud after losing her eyesight. "Go away—send my pretty little grandbaby in here," she'd hiss to the chagrin of her doting daughters. I was thirty at the time. I was a so-so daughter, but I was a spectacular granddaughter. My grandmothers were born the same year and died at age 95, within a month of each other.

Fifteen years later, I found a third. Baby brother showed me a photo. Grace was fire-haired and full-figured—like a grandma who knows her way around whole cream and butter—beaming at the camera and therefore me. Excitement bubbled through me. I had to meet her and was ready to hop on a plane to fly into her loving pudgy arms.

We'd be so precious together, like one of those little Hummel fig-urines—except broken and superglued back together, shiny along the cracks from haphazard placement and runny glue. A priceless attic find. Just blow the dust off.

"She's your family. It's up to you if you want to tell her," I mono-toned, trying and failing at inflection. After lunch, he told me to call our shared mother's best friend; he said she'd always known about me and wanted to talk.

I raced home and rang her. She was ecstatic, gushing through the phone. I was barely three sentences in when she cut me off.

"I called your Grandma." She said it like a confession, but one she wasn't ashamed of. "I sent her your photo and I said, 'Know who that is? Your granddaughter!'"

My heart again bounded, high as the rooftop.

"She says she doesn't remember your mom being pregnant, but I know she does." This lady called my birthmother "your mom," like I had a right to her, to "my" story. And she was no pussyfooter. She spilled the beans about Grace kicking my baby-bumped mother out of the house. In the winter. In Chicago. Who does that? Even in the Sixties, which by then were the almost-Seventies.

There I go again, circling back to it. I mean to let it go, and I would, could, if only Grandma Grace would talk to me. I'd let everything go, and she could too. We could just—be.

Here's the thing. It took time, almost two years after that first lunch with my brother, to figure it all out. All the while, I gave Grandma Grace her space. I held out hope she'd change her mind, want to talk, or write, or something, anything. Meantime, I kept digging through the mystery of how I came to be.

A search angel and DNA helped paint the most probable portrait of my ancestry. In the end, all evidence pointed back to the beginning—my initial closest DNA match—who was also an adoptee. He'd gotten his OBC too. It listed my biological grandparents as his parents. But his DNA only matched one side of my family, Grace's. I had a paper and blood trail to prove it.

"He must be your Grandmother's illegitimate child," my search angel said. "That's probably why she won't speak to you."

It was beyond a bullseye, and that's when it hit me: the shame of women in my family, both adoptive and biological, generation after generation. Was it a coincidence, or just being a woman? If you can't make a baby, you're shamed. If you make one at the wrong time, you're shamed. There are fifty ways to leave your lover, but countless ways to shame a woman. Maybe my new Grandma secretly feared I'd somehow find her relinquished baby. And I had.

I had a million new questions. My "birth family history" paperwork contained more blanks than information: no ethnicity, extended family details, or other medical history. There was, however, a note about a "nervous breakdown," that my grandmother was hospitalized for. In sexist 1960, that could've meant anything, but I wondered if maybe it came because of her surrendering her youngest son. Perhaps that broke her so completely that nine years later, she sent away her own daughter to a home for unwed mothers. My head was spinning.

Turns out, trauma is the chickenshit that fertilizes our family tree. It runs through our branches. Trauma begets trauma. That's what this little girl was made of. Science says the egg that became me was already inside my mother when she was inside my grandmother. Clearly, we all got a little scrambled.

Still, I waited. For Grace.

I asked my birth mom's bestie "Can you ask Grace if I can just write a letter to send to you to send on to her? You wouldn't even have to give me her address." Bestie relayed my request more than once, and more than once, the answer came back, "No."

And what would I have even written? Nothing. Everything.

I'd have written that I had wonderful parents, that I didn't want anything from her, never wanted to interfere but always wondered where I came from. I'd have asked for any stories about my mom as a little girl. I'd have told her this city baby ended up a farm girl, and isn't that funny? Isn't life so funny?

I'd have written we never have to speak of that year. Or that other year.

I'd have written it was okay she tossed out my mother and only took her back without me. I'd have written I understood it wasn't personal, though I am the person who got thrown away, so it's hard not to take it personally. It's OK, Grandma Grace—it made me tougher. I know we all have our trauma, our secrets. I understand. I get you.

I'd have told her I found her son, but he died from Covid. We were still dotting the i's and crossing the t's when it took him. I'm unsure if he ever contacted her or just took her secret to his grave. I'd offer to keep her secret too. I'm telling you her story, but my name changed with adoption, and I changed hers here too. Grace is just what I call her. To protect her and as a reminder to myself to offer her some—grace.

I've written Grace a thousand letters in my head. I've started three in real life, in earnest.

~~Dear Grandma,~~

~~Dear Grace,~~

Hey Lady,

I used my best cursive, the kind they used to teach, the kind I practiced over and over until my little fingers ached from holding the pencil too tight. I always held everything too tight or tossed it away. One or the other—never could stand the in-between. I then ripped my best handwriting and words into tiny pieces the same way we'd tear up notes back in grammar school. Don't get caught. Destroy the evidence.

Good girls don't spit, but curious girls do. I spit in a tube, and sent a bunch of forms in, and scavenger hunted my way to Grace. Proof positive. DNA doesn't lie. People do. Or so say all those witty genetic genealogists.

I don't send the letters. I don't call. I wait. For Grace. Until …

From Grace's online obituary. Edited (in italics) by me.

(Name Redacted AKA Grandma Grace), 92, of (city and state redacted) passed away on August 20, 2023. She was a loving mother and grandmother. She is survived by (names redacted) her son, her daughter, and two grandsons.

(And a granddaughter. Here's where my name would go. Right here, or maybe even before the grandsons, since I'm older. I was there first.)

She was preceded in death by her daughter *(my mother I never knew)* and grandson.

(And a son she never met. Here's where his name would go.)

Grace retired from Wrigley's Gum in Chicago, Illinois, and later worked *(redacted)*. She dedicated her career to these companies, leaving a lasting impact. *(And now I know just a little bit about her. And I google the gum plant, long since closed. I imagine her packing the juicy fruit I chewed as a girl. The spearmint I used as a teen to hide the smell of cigarettes or booze, or both. Thanks Granny.)*

No memorial services are planned at this time. In lieu of flowers, the family kindly requests that any contributions be made to any charitable organization of your choice.

(If I plant a tree for you, Grace, will it make up for the tree you took from me, kept from me for eternity?)

Our thoughts and prayers go out to family and friends during this difficult time. May her memory be a blessing to all who knew her.

Rest in peace, Grandma Grace. I'll never tell. Well, I'll always tell, but I will keep your name out of it, which is, in its own way, keeping your secret. Your name will never leave my lips, but you will never leave my heart.

I'm still waiting, with grace, for Grace.

Cathartic Heart: Ruminations

amanda suvada

Design

Veins
The Right Atrium: The Garden
The Right Ventricle: The Hallway
The Left Atrium: The Car
The Left Ventricle: The Glass Home
Arteries

Veins

We all die alone. This law extends to the heart—the one mechanism that seems to support the whole of our being: love and loss and all vitality that flows through the human frame. Most people are afraid of dying alone, of the isolation in the end. They fear the loneliness that comes with being reduced to only the self; the end that comes with that final loss of the heart, our last beating companion, and the last bated breath.

So, what makes the heart so special? Why, instead of the liver, or the small intestine, or the spleen, or any other organ, is the heart characterized as the epicenter of the self? The thing described as "good" or otherwise in one's epithet? It isn't the only vital organ in the body. The body is a holistic system—everything depends on everything else for the system to run smoothly. When in emotional pain, why do we not describe that pain as coming from the liver or the spleen? When we feel fulfilled, why do we not say our lungs are filled? It would, in fact, be directly opposed to exhaustion's impassioned sighs that leave them empty. So, what makes the heart special and such a prime choice for metonymy—so perfect for all the figurative and abstract strings attached to it? In the words of the character Edgar Allan Poe (Harry Melling) from the film adaptation of Louis Bayard's *The Pale Blue Eye*, "Well, the heart is a symbol, or it is nothing. Now take away the symbol, and what do you have? It's a fistful of muscle of no more aesthetic interest than a bladder."

The heart creates warmth. It is the locomotive engine of the circulatory system. The veins and arteries of our body let blood ooze through every fiber of our being. If you removed them and stretched them out in a singular line, they'd encircle the world several times over. The heart is the mover of vitality—not simply a foundation to support or secure it, but its influence reaches through every corner of the self. The nervous system or stomach may influence the senses, but the heart and its infrastructure are responsible for connection; for telling those around us that we are alive. Yet to be petrified. Still mortal.

Right Atrium: The Garden

"I want you to think of one good thing about that house."

It's always been the garden. The door to the heart of every home has always been in the trees and the sway of the grass. The things I've been lucky enough to grow up with, and out of, and back into yet again.

On Lakeshore Avenue, it was the Japanese maple, the daffodil bulbs, and the sappy pines next to the sign "Hutzilac Norte." The cucumbers my stepdad got upset with because he couldn't pronounce them. The chives in the garden that were my older brother's favorite. The heart-shaped flowers in a hanging basket, the huge trees just out of memory which formed the backdrop of the trains we'd race to the window to watch as they passed and followed the road below.

On Vineyard View Drive, it was the hefty pine trees rustling along the gravel driveway. The leafy something-or-other growing out of the shaded creek bed at the bottom of the hill—the most gorgeous green I've ever laid my eyes on. The bent oak tree we climbed with the neighboring kids—the one by the new fire pit and the sign "Hutzilac Muy Norte." The grass in the fields growing tall enough to shelter deer and to play hide-and-seek before the winter snow flattened it (along with our sleds and a canoe my little brother beamed out of like a searchlight on the bow).

On 143rd Ave, it'd been the arborvitaes I trimmed with my dad's tools—especially the wire cutters and needle-nose pliers. The neighbor's bluebells and fake grass. The oak trees over the driveway my dad wanted to take out for the sake of the concrete their roots twisted under. The sugar snap peas and tomato jungle spawned from my stepmom's green thumb. The tree in the backyard my stepsister and I wrote a "contract" for—as insurance that it would stay, though now sickened on one side and tilting over the split in the trunk. Our swing still hangs up on the branches. We never did mow the grass below it more than once.

"I want you to think of one good thing about that house. Just one."

Of course, it was the garden. Even as the house grew sick and the garden stilled behind my window, it was always the garden. The crabapple tree was my favorite, just surpassing the ladder-tree out front and the fragrant honeysuckle clinging to the railing of the deck.

It was lunchtime. The sun was out. I was younger then, like all of us.

Do you want a PB&J?

How could a younger brother so small and yet so rapidly grown in retrospect say no?

Alright, I'll show you how to make one, so you know how to do it yourself.

I set out a blue plate. I toasted the bread in the toaster oven with the loud dial. I took the peanut butter and jelly out of the fridge and put together the pieces.

Triangles or rectangles?

Triangles.

Triangles will taste better.

I said this jokingly. Favoring triangular sandwich halves was a novel thing for me at the time. It's funny. I now think rectangles must've tasted better. Those were the ones made for me and maybe we're not meant to change the way we cut our sandwiches. Wouldn't that make it simpler?

We sat out in the yard under the crabapple tree. The tree had bloomed recently, and the air smelled like nectar, and its limbs met small hands and feet begging to climb it.

Within the human psyche, we idealize virtue. But with that idealization, one must confront themselves when they're driven to ask if that is the true nature of humanity. Does everyone truly have the capacity to be benevolent and kind? And who's to say that kindness isn't for the self? The human being, like any animal, is hardwired for survival and reproduction. Everything else is extra trimmings and polish—the gloss one puts over the rough edges to harden and shine the heart. So, if misanthropy has such shining truth, why does humanity hold onto love and the goodness of the heart?

The desire to trust and care for others comes with the need to survive. Strength in numbers keeps people together despite trespasses and mutually inflicted pain. After all, the world was born in the image of asters and goldenrod: fields of symbiosis. The heart is not exempt from such a foundation. It is meant to support the body and the mind, which in turn have glorified the heart and immortalized it as the root of all vitality. The successful endurance of the heart and person must be mutual to exist in the first place.

What more is there to the heart of a girl? The plush interior of the beating walls, hardened and yet easy to fracture? The thing the body wraps itself around to guard and to have and to hold. There's nothing left of the things that wash away in the shower, away from a single sieve or blank page to catch anything. Everything floats away like the rapid hummingbirds at the feeder or the butterflies from my empty net.

But I'm seen by the tulip garden on the Palouse and by my grandmother's red begonias, geraniums, and roses I helped her prune. They have eyes and they glint like diamonds when the heart is under pressure. The garden was where I learned about worthiness before I ever felt the need to ask for it. The garden always forgave me.

Right Ventricle: The Hallway

Tiles and irony at the end of elementary school.

Fall mats when I was thirteen.

Carpets and stairs and a tearful confrontation when I said no and then said nothing to unhearing ears.

The entryway where I always take my shoes off.

I wonder why you'd ever bring him through the hallways of those apartments. Why you need to have a shadow. I wish you'd take a breather and scrub the fog from your eyes now rewoven into mine—the ones now cataractous and shaded by sunglasses you've supposed you ought to wear. It's something that I, like you, neglect. I know you wish your own shadow was younger, and this time he is, but he ages you. I love you and he makes me sad about it.

People talk about silver linings and the sun behind the rain cloud to make something more awe-inspiring. But I don't think suffering is a door to divine light or some great awakening. Suffering appears like a hallway stretching onward. It's a needed shelter that humanity's existential masochism calls us to. There is no ease without pain, and there is an ease in the pain itself: the release of purgatory; one's consumption and greater joy and self-actualization; the buzzing peace in the discomfort of dissociation. There's something about becoming phantasmal—beyond human meekness and yet inspired by it.

I'm afraid to run out of hurt and words to say and things to remember. I'm afraid my brain will calcify, and my heart will never beat with the same recklessness of losing. Love is mutual tolerance of pain in exchange for stitching up the wounds for each other. It's an old experience—Kavan's glass girl and he who chases her; Orwell's young rebels; Amy Winehouse: music, fame, love, femininity, abandon(ment).

Under it all, everyone wants to be stuck together while supergluing the gashes in their skin; the ones breaking through to scathe the muscle of the heart.

Left Atrium: The Car

I love to have the windows down and the music of a friend playing, jamming at the lights like someone selfish. That's joy. The heart resonates with the stereo's base. Bumping and beating, my chest is made into music and forced to move by the ephemeral, tight-gripped white knuckles beating the heart.

I'm thinking now: of you. Every one of "you."

You tell me not to kick the seat.

You're singing with Kesha as you steer. I blink. It's so quiet when you drive, until I'm standing alone in the room of my heart.

She doesn't like the car quiet. I learned from her.

I'm drifting off as I steer the truck along Utah roads, cranking out the hours and neatly lining them up. There's no water in Utah, save for a reservoir or two. I love the layers, but I couldn't handle the lack of water, and the big open spaces and valleys of rocks and dirt. I'm an evergreen state baby, and I need blue or green evermore.

Swap?

We pull over and you take the wheel so I can sleep under the bright, air-conditioned heat of summer and repressed homesickness.

Sometimes things remind me of when you were in the dim light of the passenger's seat, talking softly while my anxiousness makes my "coming in hot" driving no better. I swerve so I don't hit the yellow metal barrier.

You're a terrible navigator.

I'm laughing it off as I say this.

I climb atop the old RV, overdressed, and nearly fall through the roof.

And I'll be laughing and scribbling it all off; I'm moving it and you to the back room of my heart.

You were sitting with me when we were on the way to check out the crane by the Willamette River—the one that we climbed when it was raining.

Okay, I'm actually scared.

But I still put one foot ahead of the other until we make it to the platform, and I giggle the whole way up, nervous tension plucked like strings.

Yeah, I wouldn't have climbed up in this weather if I were you.

And you're there too, when we run the red light and go the wrong way through the intersection; but who's watching? Zip it and lock it. You're a bad luck charm and a good laugh talisman, and my happy tears well up in my eyes as I turn the wheel.

Thank you for listening to Basia with me when I park the car; then we go run in circles.

It got real when you said, "Keep in touch." That's when I started thinking of Chappell Roan playing and the sun shining down on the parking lot; when I started thinking of you flying like a flightless bird slingshotted down the tarmac at breakneck speed. That Honda Accord has pulled out of the shadow of this high school for the last time now, I'm sure; alongside the car with papers thrown in through the broken window.

Things spill out in all the funniest ways—like blood into the lungs left voiceless.

What more is there to say about the girl who never screams until the surroundings are silent? Until it can pass like a sneeze heard from the next room over above the bass and under streetlights. I don't like to feel my pulse, but I need to. When I'm sitting in the quiet driver's seat alone and so clearly out of control within myself, I ooze into the air until the heart is stripped clean. Until I can hear the birdsong outside and think until tears trickle down my cheeks, right and then left, into my lap. The lap supporting the shoulders I carry (in actuality, based on perspective) nothing on but dust. The lap sitting atop the legs that have walked five million miles. The lap that's a part of the body which rarely feels like home, despite being the only one I've ever known, and will ever own. The chirping of some winged thing continues until the beats under the layers of me for once feel like mine. Does the bird I've never seen until a few weeks back sing now? Or is it the bluejay like the ones that became my favorite because my mother pointed them out to me at least three times over, that I never saw until they were sitting up in the driveway's sheltering trees. The chirping of some winged thing continues until I can walk into the over-spilling house of my heart and hope to find a home. Until the concrete walls I hold myself in become thin as paper and fall to cover the ground for little me to cover with pale pastel chalk. I watch and smile.

Left Ventricle: The Glass Home

I want to live in a house with big, clear windows and soft curtains. One that's peaceful, albeit messy. I want to build a home where the morning sun rises and tumbles through the blinds softly to wake me, and moments feel worthy of being immortalized by a magnet on the fridge. Every word I've ever learned, crammed up in my mind, seeping through my skin, and cranked out into writing only ever has one purpose: to find home. The oftentimes rather fruitless search for a compass tends to leave me spinning like a cyclone, one cyclops' eye of mine open as I scramble to catch the thoughts in flight building my past like a cul-de-sac at the entrance to the driveway, to the walkway, to the garden, to the home of me. Not my self, but myself. The glass home seems so clear cut, but still, I struggle to wipe its opaque glass clear.

Birds hit windows. It's the nature of hope—that wonderful thing with feathers (as Dickinson and Kingsolver put it)—to fly. We're born into the cradle in the treetop, sending out dreams meant (like us) to take flight. And yet, the world spins and the wind churns until the cradle rocks so hard that gravity hits us like a sledgehammer on an anvil and we're brought down to Earth. Hope and dreams are flying cousins who we listen to singing from the trees, and watch fling themselves into the light; like propellers pulling us along through the plainness of days and nights on repeat and rewind, never unwinding. We become so spooled up, but still, we stand in place for the songs of the great martyrs and flying things with feathers, praying to catch onto them as if from a kite string.

I flew a kite over the field in the middle of the track's ellipse, but never did I ever see the hope and dreams that must've held it up on the breeze. I only ever saw its shape of a ladybug and thought of holding on.

The home of myself is surrounded by feathers. Feathers like souvenirs and unspoken goodbyes. I scrape them from the windows to see in. Disillusionment is the thing laid bare with its feathers plucked, and that is what is left standing. It and pragmatism thus form the rocks I choose not to throw but would rather use as the foundation for my glass home. That is what sets the panels at the right angle— the thing that keeps it balanced, though it shakes me from under my feet. It is what I dig under to draw up the saltwater that I need for reconciliation; the thing letting me flood the house with a fulfillment much thicker and richer than any freshwater or ever-sweet air. It lets me wrap myself in down comfort that I never would've had without the mess of feathers and things that broke.

My home with big, hazy windows and soft, thick curtains will be beautiful. It will be a place where I will sit among all the objects of myself, and it will be so solid and fragile. I'll break without brittleness or bitterness, and everything I love will polish the stones that it itself could throw inside, so that we have something else refracting the light coming in. In my glass home, I never want to forget. My skull will never bare dents and holes from failed lobotomies. The only such holes will be ones I punch in the walls like how my stepsister did in her ceiling—with avidity to make more windows and ways through.

Arteries

There's no way to go back and change things. I lay on the twin mattress in my childhood home, long overgrown with mold. Infested. A reminder that life goes on in my absence. Time's hinge creaks forward always, an ungreased one-way door. And yet, I see her dancing in this old room. The old room with the outlines on the wall left by the furniture abandoned and taken. The old room with the rotting carpet and holes everywhere—leaking. The window is open, and the rain has come in. The stained curtains are flitting in the breeze. This is the room of my soul; the small room of my heart, long overtired and washed in the glitter of nostalgia. I see her playing with her stuffed animals and her tea set. I see my mother walking through the door. I see sibling squabbles. I see others allowed in, us looking at each other with eyes glazed over. I see this mirage of magnificence and utter mundaneness in the fading November light and wonder how it's possible—why this attraction exists and why I'm brought back. I wonder if I ever left in the first place. Perhaps memories have a constant life of their own and I've been here for too long. I've been longing to be here. Maybe that's why places carry things and roofs end up sagging. Maybe the human mind can only take things one at a time—one day at a time; can only handle when things are stacked up versus thrown into a sludge-like amalgamation of life: all at once. Maybe that's why the heart sinks into such a beautiful, crumbling monument—why it decays so kindly to make way for what's left after "me." But I think deep down, I understand that living out a moment in this linear fashion still manages to make it last forever. That, or it's another thought without basis. The meandering, abstract thoughts I come up with while running my hand along the yellowing, peeling wallpaper and book pages in the dilapidated, swollen, sunken, lively house of my heart.

Tears that smell like Idaho;
A room that never smells the same.
I'd say I'm a whirlpool, but then I'd have to come down
To a point,
Not a pit—a real core
Meaning.
If we only ever see things strung out, I wonder if God sees in 3D.

Muscle Memory

harley tonelli

On our wedding day, I didn't want to do a cheesy first look with the photographer. I didn't want you to gasp when you saw me in my dress; the cheap dress I had to buy off the rack at the last minute because the fancy gown I bought the winter before was going to cost too much to be altered. I wanted you to laugh. More than anything, I loved to hear your laugh. It was so big, so too much, so surprising to hear coming out of your mouth. I told the photographer I had a plan. I was going to hide behind the grand piano, and she was going to lead you toward me so I could jump out and scare you. It wasn't an entirely new idea. On many rainy nights over the past four years, I had shocked you when you walked in the front door of our one-bedroom apartment by jumping out from behind the entryway wall. To your credit, you never got mad. You would sometimes shriek, sometimes fall to the ground. Always, you would laugh.

The locked door of your basement office. The screaming. The sound of a skull hitting the wall.

I could hear the photographer bringing you toward me, so I crouched down behind the piano and waited, my new white lace heels digging into the backs of my feet. When I saw you round the corner, I leapt out. *Boo!* You immediately started laughing, that big, beautiful laugh I loved so much. You grabbed both my hands and looked at me, taking in the hair, the makeup, the dress. You smiled so wide I could see the gap in your teeth, your molars, the one tooth you chipped in a bike accident back in college. I had rushed you to the hospital in a taxi in the middle of the Yankees/Red Sox game, blood dripping from your mouth and chin. You had such a bad concussion you couldn't tell the doctor at Mass General what month it was. Even back then, at nineteen, I knew we'd get married one day. I already loved you that much.

When I deleted the picture by the piano from Facebook and Instagram four years later, I could still see on your face how much you had loved me in that moment. I could see how loved I felt.

We had the ceremony by the little lake you grew up swimming in. It was a Thursday evening in early August, warm but not too hot. Most of the grass was still green. The water was still. There were birds in the trees that I hadn't learned to identify yet. My father walked me down the makeshift aisle, crying softly. My brother officiated. You and I read each other poems we had handwritten into tiny black notebooks. At the end, after we kissed, my brother turned toward the lake and started sobbing.

A year after the divorce was finalized, my brother got married at a summer camp in rural Vermont. I was a bridesmaid in a blue linen dress. At the end of the ceremony, I turned my white heels away from the birch arbor toward the lush New England hills and cried. I was happy for him. I counted three blue jays in the trees. I was happy you weren't there.

At our reception your dad got too drunk, like he always did, and told inappropriate stories. He commented on his daughter's weight. He told me to act more "ladylike." Your brother wouldn't talk to me at all. Not a word. He never liked me, even after I became his in-law. But my family was ecstatic. We danced and cried and laughed. I didn't let anyone take pictures of that part. I wanted it to be just for us. My best friend took a video of our first dance from under the table and sent it to me after the wedding. When I put my arms around you and Nat King Cole started playing, we looked like two people who really would be in love forever.

My parents walked in the open front door of our little house. You were locked in your office downstairs. I was lying on the kitchen floor in my maroon sweatpants, wailing. The early April sunlight was streaming through the window, illuminating the painting of the avocado you had made for me the year before. The lilac tree at the window was growing little green buds. My father knelt on the wood floor and cradled my head in his hands. I think that changes a person, seeing your child like that. I don't think you're ever the same afterwards.

At the end of our wedding night your brother drove us the forty-five minutes to our fancy hotel, dead silent. It didn't matter he hated me. Nothing would ever change how much we loved each other. We were twenty-three and time moved just for us. I peeled off my dress, still mostly white, but now with a prominent spaghetti sauce stain on the left shoulder. I chucked my shoes into the open doorway, blackened with dirt from where they had sunk into the earth by the lake. We laughed. We couldn't stop laughing.

At the hospital, before they took me away, I slipped off the rings and handed them to my dad. A month later, I took the divorce papers I filled out myself to the courthouse in a pastel blue accordion folder. The court clerk handed me the heavy stamp with the case number to mark the documents, page by page. I pressed down as hard as I could. That summer, I took the dress to Goodwill, spaghetti sauce stain and all. Where do you live now? Are you in love again? I would miss you less if I remembered you honestly.

Shadow Boxing in Lompoc

j.d. mathes

I shuffled off the bus with a clatter of chains. The prison, with its guard towers, double cyclone fences, coils of razor wire stacked rows on rows, and buildings constructed of imposing slabs of concrete, looked like a fortress to repel attacks from Medieval armies. I'd just come from Arizona, where there were fences and razor wire, but that facility had been recently built and looked like a campus for high-risk students who ditched class. Given our penchant for school "security," it was no wonder a prison would look like a school built in America at the same time. But this place, Lompoc, I was warned, was no joke. The convict ahead of me said the Falcon and the Snowman were here doing time for passing secrets to the Russians. We clinked our way beyond the armored door to intake.

After processing, they locked me into one of those narrow, old school, steel-barred cells with a bunk bed, a stainless-steel toilet and sink, and no window. My new cellmate, a skinny Cholo kid with slicked-backed black hair and a whisper-thin mustache, stood at the back of the cell to give me room to come in. He looked at me with half-closed eyes and his chin raised, sizing me up like a tailor. The guard stood behind me for a moment until the door rolled closed with a loud clang.

The bottom bunk was made and had some photos taped to the wall, so I put my stuff on the top. I said hi and he gave me a frosty "what's up nod." His stand-offishness wasn't unusual. As far as he knew, I could be from the Aryan Brotherhood or, worse, a snitch or a cop. Either way, paranoia was the default greeting. I didn't know him nor knew if he was prone to shanking a person as they took a crap.

I climbed onto the top bunk to wait for dinner. I wished I had a book to read, but I was stuck in my head. My cellmate started shadow boxing. He stood in the narrow space and jabbed, crossed, uppercut, bobbed and weaved, shuffled forward and backward, and side-to-side a few inches. I'd been learning how to box in Arizona from a professional trainer we called Cutter before he lost interest when I refused his offer to go pro after my release. My cellmate's punches were all shoulders and arms. He didn't use his hips or legs to create torque and generate power through his shoulders into his fist. It was an imitation of a boxer.

That evening, the guards marched our row to chow and then back to the cell block. I managed to get a couple of science fiction paperbacks off a book cart. On the top bunk I read as my cellmate danced back and forth, jab, jab, cross in close quarters to his body, muttering how he was going to kill a *pinche* punk.

After lights-out, I stared through the bars, across the catwalk to the big open area. In a hotel, it'd be a five-story atrium, but here it was a giant rattle-can swallowing the noise and spitting it back off the walls. At night, the lights cast a weird glow. The way they stripped the cell block making it like one of those stereographic paintings you were supposed to look at with unfocused eyes to see a hidden image. The light seemed of another era, of an old-time movie, and I watched the shadows trying to find shapes, find some whisper of something that wasn't there and would never be.

It was like when I was with the armored battalion in the desert at night. We'd set up hides and then watch the darkness, waiting for the enemy to materialize out of nothing. The sound of the guards' boot soles on concrete, and the rattle of keys as the they walked the catwalks. The odors of earth and animal manure wafted from the countryside and mixed with the bleach and smell of men washed with industrial soap. The snoring was punctuated by coughs and farts. An old man hacked so hard I heard tissue breaking loose in his lungs.

My chest constricted. I couldn't breathe well, and my heart thumped inside my ribcage. My body was rigid. I struggled to move, but I couldn't, and my muscles hurt from the exertion. A child's terror of possession, of being helpless gripped me, as if someone were straddling me, but I couldn't see them because my eyes were squeezed shut. Time was motionless in the darkness. A guard walked by and shined a light over my face. My blood pulsed through my eyelids, sweat slicked my body, and my heartbeat sped up like an over-revving engine. I considered calling out for a guard but didn't. My mouth dried and I wanted a drink of water so badly, but I didn't want to get off the bunk to reach the sink. I would bear the thirst until morning. I focused on my breathing to slow my mind and my heart. The blackness returned. Eventually, the feeling subsided. The night settled, and I fell asleep.

Days passed as I read paperback thrillers and westerns. My cellmate shuffled back and forth all fucking day, jabbing and hooking. At night he gritted his teeth and breathed like someone had forced his head into a plastic bag until he finally passed out. The fear of sleeping around strangers wanes the longer you are with the same person. For me, it was when they switched cellmates or moved me that made me jumpy again. Still, I lay awake until I was sure some accident wouldn't befall me in my sleep. My cellmate was as garden variety as carrots, as far as inmates go, and not on the edge of mayhem. It wore on me the way a small splinter stuck under your skin can wear on you.

A few days went by, and the guards ordered us to strip. With towels in hand, they marched us to the showers. We waited in two lines in front of two shower heads for our turn under the ice-cold water for two minutes of wash with soap from dispensers on the wall and rinse time. We shivered as we toweled off, and when everyone in our group had a chance to freeze in the breezeway, the guards marched our blue bodies back to our cells.

I'd tuned out my cellmate as he shadowboxed and muttered. I wondered how long I was going to be locked down with this guy, shelved on a bunk like in a sci-fi movie where the astronauts are placed in suspended animation until they arrived at their destination. Except I was conscious of time passing. It was some trick of nature to make the seconds and minutes drag. A week was gone, and I struggled to remember what books I'd read, what I'd eaten for breakfast, not knowing when the last time I showered—only recalling being naked in a line for a quick scrub, as if on a field exercise conserving water. My body remembered the sensations of days gone by, and I started to wonder if I even existed. I dreaded how many months this would drag on.

I woke with a start, catching a breath. I sat bolt upright, swinging my fists like I was drowning. The kid shook my foot just out of reach of my right cross.

"What the fuck?" he said. "That screaming gonna' bring the man. Seriously, every fucking night."

He sank back into his bunk, bitching that he always got stuck with crazy fucks.

Whatever, I thought. I'm not the one grating my teeth and shadowboxing demons.

I watched my cellmate shadowbox and debated if I should tell him how to improve his form or let it go. Did he really give a shit? Would he get pissy, act offended and try to fight me? I didn't want to have a throw down over this, but he boxed like when I was a kid, and we'd imitate Bruce Lee after watching *Enter the Dragon* or *Fists of Fury*. He went through the motions of punches, but never had any training. He'd get his ass kicked the second he squared up to a brawler.

This had been me too. I learned if you trained to fight half-assed, it'd get you creamed even if you thought you were being hard core. Before my arrest, I trained in the martial arts with my best pal and others from my National Guard unit. My first week in the county jail in Vegas found me struggling to defend myself against people who didn't give two shits about hurting or getting hurt. As a soldier, I was told to sweat more in training and to bleed less in battle. I'd sweated gallons and still bled plenty.

My cellmate reminded me of my friend Pablo from grade school, a skinny kid. We'd been in the third through fifth grades together until my parents moved us to live in the desert in southern Arizona close to the Mexican border. He once took me to his church with its ancient-looking bell tower. I had become an atheist partly from my father's Vietnam War stories filled with horror and insanity, and his railing against corrupt religions who, without evidence, commanded us to blindly follow them.

It was around the same time I'd quit believing in Santa Claus. I still loved church architecture and was curious to see the stained-glass windows with the sun streaming through them. Once inside, it was quiet and cool even though the temps were close to a hundred outside. No one was around. He led me to the pulpit where I marveled at the colored light streaming into the church. That, to me, was a miracle—to change the color of the sun and create something meaningful and beautiful with the sunrise.

The stained-glass illuminated Jesus and the Apostles feeding the poor and blessing prostitutes and thieves while chastising the rich and hypocritical. There were a lot of statues and a big one of the Virgin Mary with her blue shawl. The crucifix behind the pulpit with an agonizingly gaunt Christ in a loin cloth, bleeding from his wounds. The crown of thorns made me touch my brow. I'd never seen anything like it. I was both attracted and horrified. My mom's Methodist church had a simple cross, no statues, and very little stained-glass.

Pablo got my attention, and I followed him back down to where a bunch of candles burned. He started to blow out the candles. "Come on, man," he said and motioned for me to do the same. I hesitated. I didn't know what the candles were for, but knew we weren't supposed to be blowing them out. He looked at me like I was a pussy, so I blew a few out. Someone yelled. A priest appeared from a side door. Pablo laughed and started sprinting. I ran after him. Out the front doors, down the stone steps, and along the street as the priest followed, yelling at us in Spanish. I followed Pablo at a run with the eyes of all the stained-glass saints watching my flight from the church.

As I think back on this, I wonder if this was my first time caught up in mischief for a friend, or at least someone who I thought was a friend. It was how I ended up in prison—covering for a friend who stole a machine-gun and then trusting another friend to stay quiet about it. I never saw their betrayal coming.

Pablo also had a way of acting tough. We called him Chicken Hawk after the *Looney Tunes* cartoon character, Henery Hawk—yes, two e's. He was a little brown bird who strutted around talking like a tough guy, always saying he was going to get a chicken to eat but didn't know what a chicken looked like. Pablo always talked about being able to fight someone, but didn't know who to fight. We all had a good laugh about it, but there was something about his need to talk shit and act like he could defend himself that felt vulnerable. We reveal our terror when we're at the mercy of violent forces.

In retrospect, it's a revelation. Learning to box and earning a black belt in a martial art all originated from my insecurity and my need to be seen as someone who could handle himself. Before incarceration, I trained to fight a definable enemy—the Soviets and the Warsaw Pact or anyone aligned with them. I also trained with the idea that if I were attacked on the street, I could defend myself, but that was secondary. After my release, I saw everyone as having the potential to do me harm. I looked at people and sized them up for what their strengths and weaknesses might be. Then divided the world into people I could beat, those where it'd be close, and those I couldn't. Odd- ly, like Pablo the Chicken Hawk, I wasn't sure who I was supposed to fight. It was said after the Fall of the Berlin Wall and the disinte- gration of the Soviet Empire, the United States needed a new enemy for the American military otherwise it'd make us crazy not having a threat to train against.

In the cell the size of a grave, I felt the distance of my past close in on me as I considered helping my roommate, but there's also the vulnerability of teaching someone to be a better fighter. They might decide to turn on you. But, in a way, he reminded me of Pablo, and it'd break this tension between us for a short time. Maybe he'd keep his guard up, not sure he could trust me. I didn't know.

The bunk springs squeaked as I sat up.

"Hey, man," I said.

He turned from the wall toward me.

"Where you from?"

"Modesto. You?"

"Vegas recently."

He nodded. "Sin City."

"It was for me."

I said, "Would you like some pointers to improve your form?"

His blank look made me feel he was about to tell me to fuck off, but he said, "Cool."

I climbed down. I showed him how to stand and move like Cutter did for me. I explained how a punch started at the feet and worked its way up like a spring releasing tension.

I said, "The big fuckers can get away with pummeling people with just their arms. You're skinny, so you need to generate all the power your body can."

I taught him how to count the steps as he went through the mo- tions, and then count the punches in a combination.

"It keeps you focused on the task in mind and body," I said.

He went through the motions, counting slowly.

In basic, we trained until we reacted before thinking and instinc- tively went through the motions of fighting under attack. Sun Tzu in his 5th century BCE book, *The Art of War*, said that soldiers must be drilled and habitually trained to be well disciplined for success on the battlefield. Tzu wrote: "The supreme art of war is to subdue the enemy without fighting," and this is the most important. Once a fight starts, even the big dogs can die because chaos doesn't care what you know or how long you trained.

"After you start getting your form smooth," I said, "you need to visualize an opponent. Like, for me, I always see the guy who ratted me out."

A slight grin appeared under his wisp of a mustache. "*Pinche* punk."

Cutter drilled into me to imagine a tough opponent and how he might move and react. "Visualize the baddest motherfucker," he'd said. It's not just about what you are doing in the invisible air, but what might come at you. Sure, you can throw a wicked combination against a bag, but a person is much different. Bags don't hit back after slipping your punches. You need to get in and spar with someone. But, first, train in the basics with visual intensity.

I climbed back onto my bunk and watched him for a few minutes. His muttering of killing a *pinche* punk was replaced with a cadence of numbers. Learning how to defend yourself can give you confidence, but when taken to extremes to fill some void, it becomes toxic. It can make a person feel exposed, which creates fear, and supports laws and policies that lock up people who don't need locking up.

I read a crime novel until we went to dinner and then marched back to the cell. I stared into the shadows as the rural smells drifted in from beyond the fence. I counted the length of my inhalations and exhalations closing out the sounds of the cell block and my cellmate's teeth grinding. I slipped into an abyss.

The other thing I think about now is distance. The distance between two people when they are a few feet apart for days in a small cell. The carceral system is designed to create paranoid people and fuck with their mental health. To keep us off kilter, I suppose. A consequence designed by thinking that by being hard on someone, they can be guided into doing right. It's like believing the way to help a person with a broken leg is to break their other leg.

My cellmate wasn't a bad guy in the end, but we both had to climb over the wall of paranoia built by our society, culture, and the system. In retrospect, he was someone who was troubled and in need of counseling and guidance for whatever situation he'd come out of in the free world. In my case, the judge had ordered I be sent to a facility where I received "psychological counseling." I'd been warehoused in the county jail, then Tucson, then sent to Lompoc via Phoenix to figure out the system and hierarchies of prison alone. Not once had a counselor talked to me.

We, as a society, have adopted the approach that just because a few are irredeemable, then we must treat everyone cruelly. Many people are redeemable but are put in a system designed to torture and worsen their problems in the name of social good. This is a moral failure. Compassion and forgiveness have become signs of weakness and has stifled the value of helping others rise above their condition to make a better society. The recidivism rate is not because we are lenient towards offenders. It is because the system fails to help as many as possible.

After being released from prison, I went to a halfway house. It didn't have any counselors or facilities to ease my transition. I needed to find a way to get around on my own, find a job, and cope with the PTSD I'd developed. This led to drinking like I'd never drank before. There is a compulsion and irrationality that drives those who suffer from PTSD. I remember inexplicably finding myself getting wasted and telling myself, "this is bad" and "no place to be," but I was powerless to stop it. It's hard to explain, but also the reason outside help is required to see a person through and give him or her the tools to fight.

For me, the halfway house existed not as a place to transition but designed only to monitor my movements and punish me. Why assist a kid with alcohol addiction when we can write him up, take away his privileges, and keep him confined to an apartment? They see you need help but sit at their desks unmoved. I spiraled and crashed, recovered to rebuild a semblance of a life, only to self-destruct into madness and crash again. My life sprawled out trailing broken relationships, alcohol abuse, drug addiction, gambling, irrational behavior, rage, depression, suicidal thoughts, and I never fully trusted people.

I'm not saying my sentence was unjust. I committed crimes. But what of the conditions, the aftermath, and long recovery from incarceration that turned two years into a decades long sentence?

It is foolish to look back and pine about how my life could have been different. Life can throw other surprises at you and change the course of whatever it was you imagined. But it isn't foolish to examine moments of your life where some intervention, a hand up, would have changed a negative outcome into a positive one. A fair shot at life on different terms without being beset with addiction, nightmares, or mental health issues. Life is hard enough already for most of us. I'm not an outlier. Multiply my experience by millions of men and women and all the family members who also suffer.

After the candle incident, Pablo told me it was sin to blow them out, but it was okay. We could confess and the priest would give us penance to absolve our sin. We could be forgiven. It reminded me of the preachers saying to ask Jesus for forgiveness, but that was just between you and Him with no actual penance given. I told Pablo I didn't believe in sin, but I did believe in penance to make right a wrong you did. This was something my father, who was a judge, taught me. You have this one life to act right and be remembered for at least trying to do good in the world, as opposed to showing moral apathy or actively trying to destroy. Or worse, become the mindless many who trailed destruction behind their ignorance.

At that time, I didn't know the significance of the candles, or what it meant to believers to have them extinguished by a couple of kids. I knew asking for forgiveness was an admission of guilt and you were at the mercy of the injured party to decide what is a just atonement. Even if it goes beyond justice and becomes vindictive.

What matters, though, is that we have the courage to ask for forgiveness and that the injured party has wisdom and a sense of fairness, so the penalty equals the crime. It shouldn't be too much to hope that upon our release back into the wild, we have been given the proper counseling and the training to face life's struggles. We need the skills to defend ourselves from ourselves beyond the walls and the wire.

One morning, before light, the guards pulled me out of the cell. My cellmate looked over his shoulder from where he slept next to the wall. He gave me the "take it easy, man" nod and turned back to his pillow. I moved in a blur of fatigue. I shuffled through a dreamland as the guards marched me down the catwalk past all the other cells where men slept. During processing, everyone appeared to be ghosts shifting around me, with their flat voices speaking from another dimension. But as the sun came up, time synced, and I realized I was awake, chained in a bus, riding past the guards' eyes staring out from the tower windows. I didn't know where we were headed, how long the trip would last, or who I'd be celled with when I got there. The tires rolled on the asphalt, and I slumped in the seat, slipping into an unworried sleep.

Later, thinking about my shadow boxing cellmate, I thought of how, as a kid, I didn't realize the evolution of Henery Hawk's character. The little hawk did learn what a chicken looked like and managed to capture the towering Foghorn Leghorn. Henery wasn't a trash talking little shit. He only needed a little help from others. Then he was free.

The Things I Want from My Father When He Dies

rylee langton

The Drum

The living room was where we sat on mismatched furniture eating unbuttered, unsalted popcorn and watching movies burned from Blockbuster rentals. The family room was bleached white: walls, couch, chair, even the fireplace bricks coated with white semi-gloss. Our mutt Lucy once shat beside the fake Ficus. No one noticed until a scab formed on the carpet. I was the only one who went into the family room. Every-other-weekend at Dad's, I would sneak in and sit on my haunches at the oak, glass-topped coffee table with a large, felted drawer for displaying items.

On display, always, were Lois's Apache gifts. Lois was my grandmother, a white woman who I never met but whose memory I keep tight in a cigarette box of three or four stories, whose ashes once got in my eye because her urn wasn't glued shut, and whose silver dotted molars I have seen in my father's palm when he dug them from the ashes when I pointed into the Apache vase and said, "What's shiny in this jar of dust?" After her children had grown, Lois went to Arizona for a weekend and came back six years later. She'd been living with the Apache, huddled in an RV park as close to the rez as she could get.

Inside the glass-topped coffee table lived Lois's ceremonial animal skin drum and a suede mallet. I would scoot to the table and hold onto the drawer handles, leaning back and pretending to lose my balance. Upon falling, the drawer opened slightly, by accident, and I could worm my little arm under the lip of the table and rest my hand on the top of the drum. Only Dad was allowed to take the drum out. He would hand me the mallet saying, "Gentle, gentle…" the same way he did Lucy when he offered her a treat.

The drum was a beautiful white deerskin, stretched tight across a round frame of reeds, with the center supported by the "x" of two sticks lashed together by leather strips. My hands weren't big enough to hold the drum by the "x," so Dad held it up in front of me. Gripping the mallet in both hands, I tapped along the edge slowly, working towards the middle, gathering speed and force in a practiced spiral. Dad said the middle was too loud, so I could only beat four inches in from the edge. Sometimes, I held the smooth pine handle like a bat, wound up for the strike, then swung. Only Dad would pull the drum away. My home run would land on his chest with a muffled thump. "Gentle," he said. Six years old, and I was too strong to be trusted with family heirlooms.

To me, the woman who gave Dad this drum was formidable, tall, and beautiful, her hands calloused from whittling mallet handles and stretching skin. I thought about what it would be like to sit in the crook of her legs as her arms encircled me and she beat the drum. She would let me bring my open palm down on its center. The result would be deafening.

I created my grandmother solely from that drum, a vase of ashes, and some teeth. Until I was twelve, all they told me was that she was a nice woman who spoiled my cousin and how unlucky I was to be born the year following her death. My stepmom Veronica once told me, while tequila drunk, a story about my grandmother that my father had told her after a bottle of scotch. "Apparently," Veronica started like one relaying a rumor in middle school, "she would sit on the phone and drink all day while they were at elementary school, and instead of getting up, she would just piss herself so she could stay on the party line." She raised her eyebrows to say, "Can you believe it?" and "I'm not surprised" about the woman neither of us had ever known, a woman thirty-years dead. What I would give not to know the short story, but to hear the whole story.

The Baseball Mitt

Dad called the garage his "Man Cave" even though it was just a garage, as evidenced by my bright pink princess bike hanging from the ceiling. When he bought the bike, I couldn't use it for three years. Gotta grow into everything. I got to ride it about a year before he sold it. I had started to roam too long, too far. My outdoor toys were stored in the garage on the bottom shelf, much like my inside toys were stored in the closet of the guest room under a pile of quilts. A guest would never know a child played here every other weekend. My shelf in the garage consisted of sidewalk chalk, a jump rope, and sandcastle forms. The neighbor girl and I drew elaborate houses down the driveway, with secret entrances and pass codes: jump three times on your left foot, avoid the piranha, code 3487. Every night, Dad hosed down the driveway amid my complaint.

On the shelf above mine lived Dad's golf shoes, coated in dust and chalk, a baseball, and his baseball mitt. I sat crisscross applesauce next to the metal shelves and held the mitt, rubbing along the seams where the leather was darker, softer. Burned into the leather was "Tommy" and his childhood address. Filmore? Florence? Fremont? I used to know. I think about calling him to ask. I think about calling him less, but still often enough, like when I caught a live mouse, when the furnace went out, whenever I make a fool of myself that produces a humorous anecdote. One hundred percent of my jokes land with my father, no matter how self-deprecating. Maybe because they are self-deprecating. I don't call.

I remember the feel of the burned letters under my fingertips. When I put my hand in the glove, I could shove all my fingers to one side. Dad came out to the garage for another beer from the beer fridge, and saw me, my back to him, hiding something precious and forbidden.

"Hey, that's mine," he said.

"I was just looking." I walked towards him with the glove out-stretched.

"You look with your hands?" He didn't sound mad, territorial maybe.

I gave him the glove. "Did your dad get you this?"

He put it on instinctively and stroked the burned letters of his own name, a past life name.

"Did your dad get you this?"

"I suppose he must have."

"Did he teach you to catch?" I ran back to the shelf and retrieved the ball sleeping in one of his golf shoes.

"He must have." He had not looked up since fitting the glove to his hand. He punched its center over and over.

"Will you teach me to catch?" I asked. He looked down and saw the red-laced ball I held as close to his face as my height allowed.

"I don't see why not."

We stood in the front yard. He donned the glove and said I'd have to learn an overhand throw because underhand was for girls. When dad taught my kindergarten P.E. class for a day, he taught us all to do push-ups, girl push-ups for the girls and boy push-ups for the boys and Rylee. He rolled the ball across the close-cropped grass, and I attempted to throw it back to him. It never reached him.

I imagined scenes of Sandlot. I imagined that house I can't remember the address to. I imagined me as my father and he as his. If I were Tommy, the glove would fit my hand perfectly and my ball would sail. I imagined my father in the incubator, three months early, with the football his dad gave him, twice his size.

My grandfather, Richard Quackenbush Langton, whom I never met, whose middle name I use as a joke at parties, who left his family to start a second one, died when my dad was 24. Dick, to his friends, worked in advertising in the Sixties in Eugene, Oregon until his untimely death by drowning. Dad said he drowned on a fishing trip, saving a friend's life. But where was his life jacket? I'd ask. Out of a hero's death and a well-worn mitt, I made a grandpa. One who would tell me girls shouldn't play with fish, but who would be secretly pleased I wasn't afraid to hold one and beat its head against the side of the canoe. He'd wait for his friends to bitch about their squeamish grandsons before bragging about his six-year-old granddaughter the fish killer. I used to picture his death with pride. Him diving into the rapids to save another, then never rebreaking the surface of the water. *How drunk was he?* I wonder now.

My father revered his father. I pictured them throwing footballs and baseballs. I longed for the same repetitive play, without goal or conversation, just time spent in the role of catcher and pitcher.

There was never talk of how much my grandfather would have loved me like there was with my grandmother, but I still wanted to make him proud. My dad took me to Mexico when I was twenty, like Dick did for him. We went to his favorite restaurant, "The Shrimp Bucket," where, if tipped enough, the waiter would pour wine straight from the carafe down your throat until you closed your mouth and wine coated your face.

"Open your throat!" my father chortled. He was so happy watching the wine drip down my face; it made him proud. Did it make my grandfather proud, too? This hero with a baseball mitt, whom through my father's giggled anecdotes taught me what a split-tail was. A man who saw the Atom bomb at Bikini Atoll. Would he be proud of me? With my courage to kill and play like the boys, drink like the boys, or would he be ashamed? Ashamed of me and shamed of my father for producing another split-tail?

After less than ten minutes, Dad was done trying to teach a six-year-old to throw like a man. He replaced the mitt on the shelf and the ball to its shoe and went inside. I took the mitt back down and spread my fingers inside, punching the center over and over.

Shark Tooth Necklace

In the top drawer of Dad's dresser, there was a small pewter box filled with trinkets from a time before Tom was Dad, but still Tommy. Mom's turquoise. Dad's pocket watch. Buttons, reminders of polyester suits and wedding tuxedos. And a shark tooth necklace. Every time, under supervision, I'd pull the tooth from its place amongst buttons, while Dad told the tale of his blood brother, as if it proved he'd committed to someone. "Are you still best friends?" I asked.

"I don't think we were ever best friends, but we will always remember each other. We are blood brothers."

The shark tooth kept me coming back to the box when Dad went to mow the lawn or to the liquor store. The thin hemp cord felt worn against my thin throat and the still-sharp tooth's point excited me when it pressed to the notch in my collar bone. I tied a loose knot in the cord, the clasp long rusted by saltwater and pictured two ten-year-old boys sitting in a field after school. Tommy pricks both their fingers with his shark tooth necklace. They pressed their bloody middle fingers together till they became tacky. They lace their fingers and walk all the way home. Two ten-year-old boys, hand in hand, devoted to their friendship. The Monday after a visit to Dad's, I'd hunt for some little girl who wanted to be tied to me forever.

Once I sat, my hand over the little tooth under my shirt pressing it into skin, and watched Dad in the kitchen, hoping he'd slip and slice his finger. I would expose my tooth prick, and he would press his finger to my throat. But his knife did not slip. Instead, he noticed my sweaty little palm stuck to my neck. "What's that?" he said.

"Your necklace." I lowered my palm. "I just wanted to wear it."

He came around the kitchen island and held it in his hand. "This isn't yours."

"I was gonna' put it back."

"So that meant you could take it to begin with? Take it off."

"Will you untie it?" I turned around.

He pulled the hemp cord till it snapped. It left a hot line along my nape. Dad immediately placed it back in its pewter box, then hid the box.

More than a decade later, we sat together on the balcony of a rental cabin on Mount Hood, smoking a joint and watching the sky threaten to snow. From his breast pocket Dad pulled a pack of yellow American Spirits. His mother's brand. His sister's brand. "The fuck are you doing?" I asked him as he lit one.

"What? You want me dead anyway. Maybe I should smoke two." He took a full lung drag. I went back inside before he began to cough. Guilt pricked at my nape. He was right, is right. I wish my father was dead. I can't take him in my arms anymore, not when his hands run towards my lower back. I can't pull his sweet smell into me and feel like I did, sitting in his bathroom, watching him press a chalk stick to his shaving cuts. I'd take it from his hands and press the bloody bits to my own chin, my own upper lip.

The secret I won't tell is that I do love him. I still love him enough I want him dead. After the call, "your Dad is gone," he will waste away. Grief will only leave room for the soft stretched skin of his palms, how he would let me climb him like a jungle gym, the squeals we shared when I pressed my frozen toes to his back, the feeling of weightlessness when he picked me up to put me on his shoulders, the squeeze he gave my hand when we put down Lucy, the shark tooth necklace he bought me in Florida. After he is gone, I'm the only Langton child left, I'll have a monopoly on our blood.

There is a sepia tone photo of my dad at seventeen wearing the shark tooth necklace. His blonde hair hangs in front of his eyes and he smiles slightly, a cigarette perched on the side of his lip. I hate the photo. It doesn't look like him. It looks like me. Forty years between us cushions the features, but in that frozen moment of the seventies, it's me. My thin shoulders, my blonde hair, my nose, the eyes, the smile, it's me. I had never seen myself in him, but there I am, Tommy.

Les Toilettes de Paris

lily iona mackenzie

Some people go to Paris for the high culture, fine wine, and great food. I have no quarrel with these motives and share them myself. But during our visit to Paris, I added toilets to my list of things to see.

Why toilets?

At the Picasso Museum, my husband and I wound our way through the many rooms, following the evolution of Picasso's art, his love/hate relationship with women unfolding before us. Then we came to a room featuring one painting that covered a whole wall. In the center sat a nude female, combing her hair, on what appeared to be a commode.

Given my own life-long experience with toilets of diverse types, I couldn't help wondering about women's relationship to them. Mine started many years ago on a farm near Langdon, Alberta, Canada. I was four, and I'd just acquired a stepfather as well as a dwelling with only an outdoor toilet. Summer or winter, we found our way into that rough wooden shed with two holes and a pit where the smelly refuse ended up. Thankfully, on winter nights, we had chamber pots we kept under our beds. And in place of toilet tissue, we used leftover newspapers or magazines.

What a pleasure when we advanced to an indoor toilet. It made us feel regal. Yet I never thought much about these pleasure domes until we lived for a year at the Imperial Hotel in Calgary. I was eight, and we shared a common bathroom with everyone on our floor. Humming, twitching, and never looking in each other's eyes, men, women, and children stood in line to use this essential outlet that included a bathtub.

But it was Picasso's nude who sent me on my quest in Paris, and I spent the rest of the day exploring a few of its toilets. My first stop was the Hôtel de Crillon, the place where Hemingway's Jake Barnes from *The Sun Also Rises* went to meet Brett, the woman he fell in love with during World War I. Unfortunately, she stood him up.

A small but elegant hotel, once a palace, the bathroom I used on the ground floor was so lovely that I could have moved in. A bouquet of red roses greeted me on an entry table, and a handsome Chinese vase took over a marble countertop. Terrycloth towels were stacked near the sinks, and tiny handmade soaps so resembled confections that I almost popped one into my mouth. The room was spacious, light, and airy, the floors and counters made of marble. Mirrors seemed to be everywhere, reflecting gleaming gold faucets and light fixtures. I rested on the upholstered lounge that appeared to have started its life in an 18th century sitting room.

It wasn't easy to leave that lovely space, but my husband pointed out that the George V, another handsome hotel and one of Paris' best, would be even better. So, we made our way there. *Its* gracious lobby had everything one would expect from such a place, including gleaming marble floors that reflected numerous chandeliers and museum quality antiques.

After experiencing such a graceful entrance, I went into the women's bathroom off the lobby with great expectations, but compared to the Hôtel de Crillon, the contrast was stark. It was dimly lit, small, and smelly, but the odors weren't from fresh flowers. Instead of cloth towels, I had to use a paper towel machine, and there were no special touches like flowers and individual bars of soap. Worse, the stalls were tiny and the toilet paper rough. A great disappointment.

Ready for some nature, we then spent time in the Luxembourg Gardens. On a roll, I decided to check out the toilet there and descended to a lower level. An eccentric older woman, whose frizzed grey hair shot out as if she'd been electrocuted, oversaw it. Sweeping furiously, she cleaned up leaves that dropped from several green plants near the toilet's entrance.

When I reached her, she called out, "Deux euro cinquante" and emptied her dish so I could add my coins. Then, she pointed me to a toilet at the end of the row. I was surprised and touched at her attempts to dress the place up. A vase of yellow daisies sat on the counter, and art prints hung on the walls, some a tiny postcard size.

But none of this prepared me for when I left the stall and ran into an Asian man standing in front of the mirror combing his hair. I wasn't used to sharing a bathroom with unfamiliar men, but I later discovered that unisex toilets were becoming trendy. Though this toilet was dingy, despite Madame's attempts to civilize it, the place was clean enough. I said, "Au Revoir, Madame," as I left, and she said, "Au Revoir," still sweeping around the plants and muttering to herself.

Ready for another perspective, I used a street toilet. It looked like a space station waiting to levitate. I put my two euros in the slot. The door slid open, retreating around a curve. The throne, visible to all, was waiting. I entered, glancing around. The floor and seat were wet because it automatically disinfects the place after every use. But I was relieved when the door closed, giving me a little privacy.

I felt vulnerable and self-conscious as I had so many years ago in the Imperial Hotel's community bathroom. In the heart of Paris, I sat on a toilet in the middle of a street, listening to people walking by and talking. Clearly, they could also hear me doing my business. A sign said I had a maximum of fifteen minutes, and I tried to use up as much time as possible by looking at the cream-colored walls and investigating the other features. Above the toilet, there was a recess in the wall. If I inserted my hands, water dribbled out. Not enough to take a quick shower or even cleanse my hands. I was getting nervous because I could hear the line of people waiting outside, mumbling in multiple languages. When I flushed, the door swung open, fully exposing its interior and me. Then another patron entered, and it once more went through its cycle.

Picasso's painting had sparked my informal survey of Paris toilets, but he isn't the only artist whose work has highlighted women in such intimate surroundings. It makes me wonder why many males associate females with them. Of course, when we use a toilet, our genitals are exposed, so there could be a sexual innuendo. Also, toilet bowls and sinks do call up images of female wombs. Maybe only the trip handle and water faucets have phallic connotations.

The term toilette/toilet itself describes the process of washing and personal grooming, activities we tend to associate more with females than with males, though in recent years, some men spend as much time as women caring for their appearance. Still, the toilet does feel like a female domain, and we women do spend more time on our "toilette" than most men I know. In the one I share with my husband, my toiletries dominate, taking over all available cupboard or counter space: lotions, special soaps, multiple shampoos. The list goes on. So, when we enter that shared space, that public space, we tend to make it *our* space as well.

To Have and Not to Hold

grey traynor

I used to wonder what it would be like to be the girl of a boy who wore a leather jacket. A guy with brooding eyes, greasy hair, and a sneer that only I could see through. What it must be like to be loved at arm's length by someone who could not go all the way, even if a deeper part of them wanted to go further. When I wanted to go further.

In my preteen years, I would imagine romance, or something like it, just off the beaten path, where the brambles lace, and flowers with stubborn roots are inedible. And when I got older, I found that prickly love, over and over; the kind that's as nourishing as salt water.

In a way, I discovered what I'd been searching for; I manifested men who might love me but didn't necessarily like me or didn't want to like me.

I've been told that I'm quick to bond with people, but I've never understood what else I'm supposed to do when meeting someone. I try to stay engaged, listen and learn. This quality doesn't make me special, but it does mean I try. Everyone is interesting because everyone's different; every shade exists even though it's impossible to bear witness to them all.

And this kind of loving attention that I implement has led me to trouble because I don't always see the spikes, the points, the stinging nettles of certain people when I'm running at them full speed for a hug. Which some people are glad for because they want to pierce skin, whether they know it or not.

The sharpness of others, of quasi-lovers, for me, at least, has always come in the form of addiction. Every. Time. I have a familial history with alcoholism, so you think I'd be able to spot an addict even when they're telling me that they "can stop at any time" or they're just having a fun summer. But why would I want to turn my back on a new friend, someone who likes bad horror movies like I do and reads obscure books? Always I believed the good would outweigh the bad, that these new friends would want to hold onto our electric chemistry and engaging times. But what unrecovered addict can promise a rose garden, when they've never known one themselves, finding only a few stray red petals crumpled under a pile of tallboys, drained and crumpled?

If these friendships had ever held or their addictions quieted, these relationships would never have gotten fuzzy, moving toward a romantic territory. But they did—none of them ever stayed clear and platonic. Maybe my love was a new thing they would allow themselves to covet and get high from. Maybe their stunted love existed as my addiction.

A month into all these relationships, all completely random men who soared into my life, who I never sought out, things would begin to get strange. Casual friendship would snowball into intimate texts, midnight phone calls, constant hangouts, gifts, acts of chivalry, curious fellow acquaintances grilling me about the "nature" of the relationship. Saying "I love you" to one another.

This behavior would build, and I would find myself getting pulled into something I hadn't anticipated. I had never had close male friendships. Was this what they were like? Why did they feel dizzying like an open secret, why did these men talk so close to me and why did I want their breath, often tinged with a sour scent of tobacco, spewing across my cheek?

The next stage of these relationships would be "the vacation," where we parted because they had to go, or I had to join my family somewhere. The calls, texts, and the hang outs would stop being so regular and urgent. But we would promise to pick up where we left off because that's what pals do; they don't let temporary distance change the dynamic. A brief time apart is certainly no big deal.

And as if it were planned, like they all knew each other, during these partings I would receive, late at night, high moons blazing, humbling texts like this: "I miss you" and "I've never met anyone like you."

Reading this, I would feel a charge like I'd been dropped in a rolling tide without even a flicker of pain and, phone to my chest, I would call it being loved.

Then when I'd get back from the trip or they'd return, I'd expect a fanfare, greedily anticipating what other glowing things they would say about me and how I was someone to admire and obsess over.

But the vacation stage was the apex, with the bubble bursting soon after. The texts would dry up. Phone calls would be ignored. Any chance of hanging out pushed away. In one instance, the guy had been home for a week before his friend told me as much. "Sorry, ha ha, I forgot to tell you. I'm back, I'm just hella busy." Those who recently spewed adoration suddenly didn't have time for me anymore. They left the party early, taking my presents with them.

I, of course, responded like any desperate lab rat would, fretting over where my maze-finishing treat had gone, texting them more than ever, trying to get any little moment of their time. This only drove them further away until it felt like I was screaming at the back of their heads. At this point, I was left with the only question someone like me in this position would have: "What happened?"

They'd say:

"Lol what?" and "Nah it's not like that" and "I don't know what you're talking about, dude."

More and more dismissal on their parts until something unspoken broke and the promise of what we had suddenly were just possibilities floating high up into the air, dissolving. This would lead us down to the final pass, where a small fire becomes an inferno only to dwindle to charred nothing, where an ant sees a shoe heel falling closer and closer.

Yet, still, I would follow their aloof leads, pretending our "friendships" hadn't changed and maybe a friend of theirs would invite me to a party. Maybe they'd happen to be moving away and having a goodbye hangout?

Whatever the scene, in every scenario came the end in the form of a "hand," twice physical, once figurative. The physical ones made their way over to me at a party, always finding their unsolicited, nonconsensual way to my ass or crotch in a crowded room, always nearby some poor girl they just happened to start dating. They never said anything while they groped me, they simply exhaled the tobacco breath in my ear, a sort of moan.

The other "hand" came as a random dressing down, a textual violence in the middle of me asking if he'd like to chill, only to have him reply: "You make me feel like shit and I'm tired of feeling like shit when in reality I could just never speak to you again and probably feel happier."

To this day, I've never had anyone degrade me the way he did, but, as the saying goes, "alcoholics don't have relationships—they take hostages."

However, this is where I get lucky because I never looked back after these instances. That's not to say I never spoke to some of them again, but in every situation, I thankfully allowed the scream of their behaviors to light up the scenario for me, a sort of spotlight where I could see the dynamic from all angles and ask myself in an embarrassed whisper, "What am I doing here?"

I hadn't found love. These were no partners or boyfriends or lovers. They were toys as broken as me, taking out their brokenness on anyone who would give them the time of day. And I had given it to them. I had let them believe, let myself believe, what they needed was a hopeful friend when that was what I needed myself.

I had to believe against what I knew, betting against the leather jackets and smug sneering that I could find someone who could be loved. Someone who understood the game, the real one, was about take, as well as give. You are allowed to root for someone, but you cannot save them, and should you want to, make sure you know how to save yourself.

I'm happy to say that I don't venture down those roads anymore. I no longer understand the point. I think these experiences amounted to fear, fearing the real thing, wanting to keep things play-pretend. Because the honest version is an open, vulnerable, substantial thing; it doesn't "resemble" anything but what it is. It's the difference between "talking" and "conversing," one is a game of overlap, and the other is two parties doing their best to show up for themselves and one another.

Madonna once sang: "Pain is a warning that something's wrong." And with the help of experience, reflection, time and doing the wrong thing again and again, I came to understand that the presence of "hurt" doesn't validate love, it's telling you that it's gone or that it was never there.

Issue 14 Contributors

Faith Allington (she/her) is a writer, gardener and lover of mystery parties. Her work appears in literary journals such as *Mslexia*, *The Fourth River Tributaries*, *Honeyguide*, *Crow & Cross Keys*, and *Crab Creek Review*.

Hannah Andrews lives and writes in San Diego. Her work has been performed onstage at the 2021 San Diego Memoir Showcase and published in print anthologies including "Shaking the Tree: Vol. 5," and 2024s "A Year in Ink."

Maria L. Berg's poetry has appeared in *The Gateway Review: A Journal of Magic Realism*, *Heron Tree*, and *Auroras and Blossoms*. She is an active member of the Academy of American Poets, dVerse Poets, and PNWA (Pacific Northwest Writers Association). When not writing poems and participating in workshops, she plays many instruments, and enjoys light-forming abstract photography, fabric art, and brisk swims in the lake.

Elizabeth Duran picked up a writing pen in her left hand when she was five, and never put it down. When she was seven years old, she wrote two stories about a car accident that put her entire family in the hospital. One was funny. One was not. It sparked a love for words that would lead to a bachelor's degree in creative writing from the University of California Riverside.

Kirk Glaser's poetry has been nominated twice for the Pushcart Prize and appeared in *The Threepenny Review*, *Nimrod*, *Chicago Quarterly Review*, *Catamaran*, and elsewhere. His poetry collection, **The House That Fire Built**, will be published in 2025 by MadHat Press. Awards include an American Academy of Poets prize and University of California Poet Laureate Award. He teaches at Santa Clara University, where he is Director of Creative Writing and Faculty Advisor for the *Santa Clara Review*.

Katie Humphries was born and raised in Florida but has lived in the Pacific Northwest with her husband and children for over twenty years. She holds an MFA from the Rainier Writing Workshop (Pacific Lutheran University), an MAT from Georgetown University, and a BA from Davidson College. Her short fiction has been published in *NiftyLit*, *Grande Dame Literary Journal*, *Tomahawk Creek Review*, *Tahoma Literary Review*, and *Gold Man Review*. She teaches English at Highline College. www.katie-humphries.com

Julie Johnson is the author of *In Another Life*, awarded the 2016 Foreword Indies Gold Prize for Fantasy, the eco-lit ode to Ireland *The Crows of Beara*, numerous short stories and essays, and a crime novel now on submission. Working by day as the Finance director for a non-profit publisher, Julie makes her home on the Olympic Peninsula of northwest Washington state with four cats, seven chickens, a Labradane, and a painter. www.juliechristinejohnson.com

Rylee Langton is a PNW-born writer with a B.A. in Creative Writing from Western Washington University. Her work has appeared in the *Scarlet Leaf Review* and *Leaves of Ink*. Rylee lives in Ferndale, Washington, with her fiancé and dog Rusty.

Saundri Luippold is an undergraduate student at Azusa Pacific University (APU), studying English and Spanish. Her poetry has been published in *Foreshadow* magazine, *The West Wind* (APU's literary journal), *Big Wing Review*, *The Charleston Anvil*, and *Waymark*. She writes on a personal blog, which can be found on Instagram @newromanticism13.

Lily Iona MacKenzie has published four novels (*Fling!*, *Curva Peligrosa*, *Freefall: A Divine Comedy*, and *The Ripening: A Canadian Girl Grows Up*, a sequel to *Freefall*), two poetry collections (*All This* and *California Dreaming*) and a chapbook (*No More Kings*). Shanti Arts Publishing released her memoir *Dreaming Myself into Old Age: One Woman's Search for Meaning* in September 2023. She also teaches creative writing at USF's Fromm Institute for Lifelong Learning and blogs at https://lilyionamackenzie.com

J.D. Mathes grew up a feral child in the deserts of the American Southwest who loved to read library books and take photographs. He is a 2019-2020 PEN America Writing for Justice Fellow, a Jack Kent Cooke Scholar alumnus, an award-winning author of four books, photographer, screenwriter, and arts reporter. Although Mathes still struggles with subject-verb agreement and where to put commas, he is finishing work on his memoir *Of Time and Punishment.*

R. G. Mint is an English teacher in Seattle, Washington. When he isn't in the classroom, he often stays busy writing stories aimed at thrilling, unsettling, or provoking thought in his readers. He is passionate about shedding light on diverse perspectives and harnessing the power of writing to bring about positive change. You can follow him on Instagram at @r.g.mint.

J.A. Nicholson lives in the San Francisco Bay Area and has degrees from the University of California and University of Florida.

Cassady O'Reilly-Hahn is a poet with an MA from Claremont Graduate University. He is an editor for *Foothill: A Poetry Journal* that highlights graduate student voices. He works for Deluxe, a company that localizes TV and Film for a global audience. In his free time, Cassady writes Haiku for his Instagram @cassady_orha. Cassady currently resides in Redlands, California, with his fiancée, Anabelle, and their two pugs, Wyatt and Jasper.

Zachary Paul is a father, husband, schoolteacher, and poet. Originality from the Oregon Coast, he has since moved inland.

E. Peregrine (they/them) is a trans/nonbinary conductor, poet, and teacher with deep roots in the Pacific Northwest. Their writing has appeared or is forthcoming in *Roanoke Review, Variant Literature, smoke and mold, Bluestem Magazine,* and elsewhere. Follow their work on Instagram at @tonus.peregrinus.

Dr. Raji Pillai is a literature and theater critic for San Francisco Bay Area South Asian news outlets, including *India Currents* for which she received a 2023 California News Publishers Association award. Her writings are at www.rajiwrites.com. In a parallel life, she works as a scientist. "Kite" is her first published work of fiction. She is working on more short stories and a novel.

Amanda Suvada is seventeen-year-old young woman, born and raised in the Pacific Northwest. Erring on the sentimental side, if she were ever caught in a house fire, she'd save: her scrapbook of a journal (written in with blue pen, mostly), her small collection of family photos, and her beat-up paper copy of *Catcher in the Rye*. "I have no real idea of what I'm doing, but that's the fun part," she says.

Harley Tonelli is a poet, musician, and lawyer from Seattle, Washington. Harley is currently an MFA candidate at the University of Washington Bothell in the Creative Writing and Poetics program, and has previously studied at the University of Washington School of Law and Berklee College of Music. Harley is passionate about birds, the ocean, and everybody getting free.

Grey Traynor is a transfemme, nonbinary writer and library assistant who has been published in Time Out San Francisco, Beacon Quarterly, Thought Catalog (Jonathan Gray), Doubleback Review, and The Purposeful Mayo. They are currently querying a horror manuscript and can be found on Instagram @greytraynor

Zac Walsh is the author of *An End of Speaking* and *Love in the Utmost*. His work has appeared in journals such as *Stonecoast, Caustic Frolic, Calliope, Gold Man Review, Last Leaves, Blue Unicorn, LUMINA, Gulf Stream, Cimarron Review, Oakwood, Alligator Juniper, The Awakenings Review, The Other Journal, Inscape, Big Lucks, Lime Hawk, Spectre Magazine, the DuPage Valley Review* and *The Platte Valley Review*, as well as in the anthologies *Extrasensory Overload, Blood on the Floor* and *Small Batch*. He lives in a small, unincorporated town in Oregon with his wife and a very old dog.